> ATTEMPT ON GALL FAILED IN
> MONTSERRAT. IMPERATIVE
> SAME MISTAKE NOT BE MADE
> DOMINICA. HE IS BIG C
> FROM WASHINGTON'S D.C.
> MAN. WHOLE PROJECT IN
> JEOPARDY. DO NOT UNDER-
> ESTIMATE.

It took a lot of Gall to intercept that message. Joe might have been flattered. But he was a pro; he also knew the danger of underestimating the enemy.

This time the enemy was very special, a big one that had gotten away. Joe couldn't lose him again—and live to tell about it.

THE
FER-DE-LANCE
CONTRACT

Philip Atlee

A FAWCETT GOLD MEDAL BOOK

Fawcett Publications, Inc., Greenwich, Conn.

*"The bright day is done
and we are for the dark . . ."*
WILLIAM SHAKESPEARE

THE
FER-DE-LANCE
CONTRACT

The island of Antigua is

a sunbaked poorhouse except for a few tropic beaches that have been appropriated by foreign millionaires and resort hotels with astronomical prices. Mercifully my plane from Kingston arrived at midnight and I was spared the sight of the seared acreage. I was not, however, spared the enthusiastic shearing given by Antiguan taxis, which are the most expensive in the Caribbean.

It was part of my cover that I had no reservation on Antigua and no continuing ticket out of it. British West Indian Airways had noted this lack, and made me sign a voucher for it, before I could board their big jet in Kingston. A few bored Americans and Canadians had deplaned with me but were whisked through customs and into chauffeured sedans. I was left alone with the black customs staff, and after I had snarled at a bare-footed Negro boy who nearly dropped one of my

9

bags, the dark official faces observed me impassively.

I looked the part. A big Yank with sunbleached hair, not bothered recently by a barber, wearing a garish sport shirt and Bermuda shorts. Add the look of a once-good heavyweight going to paunch, with a Polaroid 360 slung around his neck, and you've about got it. And, naturally, this American clod is short-tempered because it is still hot at midnight in the customs' shed of Antigua's Coolidge Field.

I dropped a few more surly remarks as the inspectors pawed through my luggage, and that made them open even the aspirin bottle. When the polite chief inspector asked how long I would be on the island, and where I was proceeding from it, I said I would stay as short a time as possible and that I had no continuing passage booked to anywhere.

"Why did you come then, sir?" he asked reasonably.

"Some friends said I should try the action at the Marmora Beach casino."

He nodded. Marmora Beach had the only casino on the island. Its inn was operated by a large American chain, but all the personnel below manager and accountant were Antiguans. The casino was run under separate contract by some Italian types from Miami; Lansky was supposed to be the shotgun back of the operation. The customs inspector noted that I was carrying $5,000 U.S. in traveler's checks, chalked my bags as passed, and observed in silence as I haggled with the most vociferous of the cab drivers, a fat black clown wearing a torn straw hat.

The price to Marmora Bay, he insisted, was $12 U.S. I replied with some heat that this was ridiculous, and we settled on $8. While we were hoisting my bags into his ramshackle car, I put the needle to him, too, and he stopped and walled the whites of his eyes. A barefoot old man drove a small donkey by us, walloping the tiny beast on with the flat side of a worn cutlass. As I got in beside the silent driver, I reflected that if I played my cards just right in Antigua, I might get my head sheared off by one of the sabrelike instruments.

It was nearly one in the morning before the cab pulled up before the luxury hotel. Even at that hour its terraces were blazing with lights. I got out of the car, watched my luggage unloaded, and tried for twenty minutes to get a U.S. $10 bank note changed, or a $20 American Express traveler's check. The desk clerk was a sullen black youth, dressed neatly in black trousers, white shirt, and dark tie. He insisted that he had no change, either in U.S. money or Biwee (West Indian) dollars.

The fat lout of a cab driver was leaning over the desk beside me, smiling faintly.

"Look, Jack," I said harshly, "I can hear the roulette wheels whirring and the slots being cranked in there. You can't run that kind of shop without cash, can you?"

"I have no change, sir," repeated the ebony lemur behind the hotel desk. Since the rooms started at $50 U.S. a day, I knew he was lying. I walked into the casino and located the pit boss, a small thug with a pockmarked face, named Sid. No, he could not furnish change; the hotel and casino were entirely different operations.

I nodded, went back to the hotel desk, and gave the sneering cab driver the $10 bank note. He departed without thanks, and I registered and was shown to a suite in the south wing. Each unit had its own air conditioning machine and terrace, and the bathrooms were enormous. When I asked the bellboy about room service, he said there was none, for either food or drink. He was just going off duty, in fact.

He shifted, unsmiling, from foot to foot, and I took pleasure in reminding him that because I had been unable to get change, his dash was out the window. He nodded and withdrew, a picture of dark dejection. I showered, dressed again, and went down to the dining room, which was on three levels. An ornate bar on one side and a bandstand on the other, with elaborate hanging lamps made of wicker amphoras.

A five-piece group in gaucho costumes were troubling the chilled air with a pounding beat. They were billed as Herman and The Mexicans, and a frenetic fat boy I took to be Herman was shouting lyrics and trying to organize an affair with the mike. Obviously untroubled by a score, he pranced around in erotic, pear-shaped glee. I ordered a Cutty Sark with soda, got one with ginger ale, procured a combination ham-and-cheese sandwich to take back to the room, and prowled the floodlit, poinsettia-spattered premises until I found an ice machine.

Thus secured against famine, thirst, and the hostile black population, I drank a pint of Mount Gay rum I had bought in Kingston and ate the sandwich. It was superb, and had a side order of souffléd potatoes. The air conditioning unit was of British manufacture and chilled the suite admirably. As I flaked out in the huge bed, I realized I would be able to play my nasal catarrh when I woke up.

I had breakfast on the windy terrace, gazing down across the sweep of crescent beach. It was fringed by cabbage palms (called in the brochure "Royal Palms"), thatch-roofed huts, and reclining lounges. To my left, below, was an open-sided bar, and just beyond it a black boy in shorts was oiling a whale-bellied tourist. His wife, also stout, was in a beach chair beside him, staring out to sea from under a feathered straw hat. In short, fake Polynesia.

The sand was grayish, but the water paled from light green in the shallows to emerald and indigo further out, and gentle waves creamed up and back across the beach. Beyond were only sun-seared hills bearing sparse vegetation.

The coffee was good, Blue Mountain from Jamaica, and I had two cups. Sipping, I meditated again on the frieze of sullen black faces I had encountered last night. I knew the faces were permanently set in that image, but my caustic remarks had not lightened them any. And the remarks had been deliberate. Coupled with this fact was another; the *Federal Palm,* one of two light cruise ships given to the Caribbean Islands by Canada, was due in Antigua this morning. She would be sailing for Montserrat at 2 P.M.

And I had to be on her for the continuing journey to Dominica, St. Lucia, Barbados, St. Vincent, and St. Sauteurs. In the last-named port, I might or might not get off; I would be notified if the agency wanted me to go on to Trinidad, the *Federal Palm's* last and home port on the southern cruise that had begun in Jamaica.

The section of the agency that is in the counterspying business had contracted me to ferret out some dark fellows who were planning considerable Caribbean mischief. The chief among these connivers, I had been told, worked as assistant purser on the *Federal Palm.* His name was John Ratoon, and if the reports were true he had an ideal spot for such machinations. Every week he went up through the islands, from Trinidad to Jamaica, and the next week his ship worked back down again.

The mischief he was allegedly ramrodding was startling and imaginative. He and his cohorts, well-hidden on the various islands, planned to seize, on a date unknown to us but imminent, all transportation and communications facilities in the Caribbean Sea. All planes, cruise and freight ships, interisland schooners, and private yachts were to be boarded and taken simultaneously. All radio and cable installations were to be seized also, including radar and weather stations. The only islands to be excluded from this take-over were Haiti and Cuba.

The airlines affected would be Pan American, Delta, Braniff, British West Indian Airways, Air Jamaica, Lufthansa, KLM, SAS, Liat, and Caribair. The surface vessels of Cunard, Fyffes, United Fruit, Booth, Harrison, Saguenay, Geest, the two flagships of West Indian Shipping Service, *Federal Palm* and *Federal Maple,* and any other cruise ships or combination boats in Caribbean ports on the target date would be taken over.

At first the idea had seemed grandiose and even ridiculous. But after several months of patiently checking out reports, mostly from the agency's in-depth plants through the islands, the higher echelons stopped smiling. Somebody was doing a hell of an organizational job.

There are over fifteen million blacks in the Caribbean Islands, and each of the lesser islands has a shaky and ineffective government with only a token constabulary. The proposed Federation fell apart several years ago. This is natural enough; these individual governments have not had time to educate officials or train armies. Even if they had had the time, they do not have the money. A complete paralysis of their transportation and communication facilities would cause a monstrous jam-up of their lame economies. Famine would be one immediate result.

And if the plotters also struck at Jamaica, Barbados, and Trinidad, large islands with modern economies and trained troops, that step would be headlined in every newspaper in the world and put implacable pressure on the British, Canadian, and American governments . . .

The trouble so far, the Black Power uprisings and invasions of Caribbean universities, had been minimal, limited mostly to Jamaica and Trinidad. But the ferment was spreading swiftly. One of the strangest aspects was a Jamaican sect called the Ras Tafarians. These odd characters were only marginally involved, but if a real break came they would rally to the barricades with confused enthusiasm.

The Ras Tafarians were unwashed hippie types sporting corkscrew curls and raffish beards. They lived, fittingly, in the Dunghill slum section of Kingston, were strong on smoking ganja, dreaming, and bombing other people's property. They got their name from the title of Haile Selassie when he was crown prince, and viewed the Ethiopian emperor as divine and ageless. One of their tenets was that they could share his immortality by a pilgrimage to his kingdom.

This connection was hard to make, because the Ethiopians are Coptic Christians, and thus seemingly had little common ground with the Gullah adherents in the Jamaican slums. But there it was. Not long ago, a merchant vessel from Ghana had docked in Kingston, and Jamaican police had to cordon it off to prevent the unkempt Ras Tafarians from boarding her by force. They angrily proclaimed that the ship had been sent to take them on the first stage of their pilgrimage to Ethiopia.

The incident was ordure, of course, except that nothing is ordure if enough people believe it. Rebels in Guatemala had carried out the ritual murder of the West German ambassador, Count von Spreti. Insurgent forces had demonstrated in Guyana, and the Black Power firebrands in Port of Spain, Trinidad, had burned several Canadian branch banks and terrorized a Roman Catholic archbishop. Most exotic of the dissident elements was a band of fifteen miniskirted Co-

lombian lasses who had broken jail and commandeered
police machine guns and four Land Rovers in their
dash to mountain freedom.

My job was to act as a *provocateur,* to create such
a disturbance at the elegant Marmora Beach Inn that
I would be forcibly deported, put on the *Federal Palm*
that afternoon as a known racist and troublemaker. So
I had a last sip of the good coffee and reflected that I
might manage it, if I didn't get killed in the convincing
process.

I put on my bathing trunks, my fashionable blue
terry cloth jacket with the wide patch pockets, and
sauntered down to the swimming pool of the Marmora
Beach. The poolside was crowded with bathers and
servants. The news had gone abroad, and none of them
glanced at me as I stalked by and staked out a place
on the far side of the blue pool.

The pool of the Mar-

mora Beach Inn was white tiled, with blue water in it, on a terrace high above the sea. On the far side was a colonnaded area with metal tables and reclining chaises, and the seaside wall was made of glass panels, opened to let the breeze through. Beyond it, the variegated waters of the Caribbean Sea sparkled with incredible green shallows and blue depths.

I spread my towel on the far side of the poolside concrete, fetched a small metal table from under the colonnade, and as I put my cigarettes, lighter, and holder on it, counted the house. Close to fifty people, about half white, and I reflected that the black ones must be in on some kind of due bill. They were too young to stand the Marmora's stiff tariff. A number of English couples, looking odd and aloof, trying to ignore the whole trying thing. I smiled grimly at that. *Just hold the phone a sec, Your Lordship,* I thought. *Whitey is about to recover his dominance.*

Several tables of heavily tanned breakfasters I made as yachtsmen and their wives from the Nicholson place in Nelson's Harbor. At a number of others, screaming sport shirts announced the presence of the big butter-and-egg men from the Middle West, or a reasonable counterfeit, the wives having unbelievable brassy or dead-white coiffures. Eighteen-year-old hair framing fifty-year-old faces. Behind me and slightly to the right sat a massive black man surrounded by his fat wife and four carbon-copy children. *Government minister,* I tagged him, or *professional man.*

Sullen black boys like the ones who had put the boots to me last night stood around in their neat black pants, gleaming shoes, and white shirts, but when I tried to catch the attention of one of them he was always looking the other way. That was no problem; I cut loose with a two-fingered, ear-splitting whistle I had learned on the island of Gomera in the Canaries. They whistle news across mountains on that island.

The hum of breakfast conversation ceased. Black and white alike turned their stares on me, with only the yachtsmen laughing. When the sullen waiters did not move, I gave it to them again, an octave higher. That jarred some eardrums and brought one of the boys slouching over. I told him I wanted a double Cutty Sark on the rocks, and to keep his cotton-picking fingers out of it.

As he moved toward the bar, beyond the two arching palms with their fronds slatting in the breeze, I glanced toward the circular, unsided coffee shop just beyond, and at the lobby across from it. Several more hotel employees, all black, had moved into view and were looking toward the pool. The news was spread-

ing; the offensive white cat in 223 was having a double, neat.

A large bundle of elegant rags came ambulating by
me and took a chair in the sun close by. There was a
meager figure inside the bundle, and after it had
plumped into the chair and begun shedding some of
its outer garments, it turned into an elderly English lady
with skin like cured leather. Beady eyes stared at me,
and the crone said, "G'morning, g'morning, lovely day
izzn'tit?"

"Superb," I admitted, and the apparition stood in-
completely revealed in a bathing costume that must
have come from a Victorian museum. It was a bathing
costume, not a swimming suit, and its wearer looked
like Beatrice Lillie after a long and debilitating illness.

"We shall have rain before noon, y'know," the old
lady announced, and I nodded respectfully. I do not
know where they come from, these fustian old English
females, but you encounter them all over the world.
Alone, self-contained, and completely assured, they
move decisively through the swarms of tourists and local residents, and I had often wondered if they were
relics of colonial servants, Sussex grandmothers visiting married daughters in far climes, or just what. Perhaps big, and wise, hotel managements employ them
as shills, and shunt them about the world on a circuit,
from Bali to Timbuktu.

My drink came, I signed for it, and under the covert
gaze of the poolside and lobby watchers, slugged it
down in one. The old British dame was sitting with her
withered legs propped apart, and a spotless handkerchief draped over her head.

"Not quite the thing, young man," she rebuked me,
but without heat. "Far too early. I told Gerald that
for thirty years."

"Oh? Liver got him, eh?"

"Terrible thing," she admitted. "He was in great pain at the end. Couldn't hold wind or water, y'know."

I nodded, distressed at the painful demise of Gerald, of whom I wot not, and uncoiled and went knifing into the pool. I did four laps in it, two with a faster crawl than they had ever seen, and another two with a thrashing backstroke that left the water churning. When I came eeling back over the edge and stretched out on my towel, the old lady spoke from under her kerchief.

"Fancy that! You looked so lumpish before. No telling about you Yanks."

"Thank you," I said. It was time for Phase Two, so I cut loose with the ear-splitting whistle again. The black boy was quicker off the mark this time, and I ordered another Cutty Sark double on the rocks. The black face withdrew, and over his shoulder I saw a white man in a business suit come out of the office beyond the hibiscus bushes. He was either the manager or the accountant; the hotel had only two white employees, both from stateside.

When the waiter came back with the drink, I managed to jab the small tray from underneath, and the glass with the ice cubes and Scotch fell off and smashed on the concrete. I counted three and began to curse him. The sound of my anger had no competition; it penetrated all the way to the front desk and the watching manager or accountant.

The young waiter stooped and began to rake the glass shards and ice cubes back onto his tray. I curtly ordered him to fetch me another drink, that I had no intention of paying for the one his stupidity had spilled. Kneeling, black skin taut over his Gullah cheekbones, he nodded, and went walking back toward the bar.

Not even the permissive yachtsmen were laughing now. The poolside had fallen silent, and most of the people gathered there were watching me without appearing to. I had gone from a diversion to an insistent pain-in-the-ass, and they felt that something would have to be done about me.

"Quite right, too," said the old English lady. "The beggars will *not* take care. Is that a flame-of-the-forest tree there beside the bar, young man?"

"One of them, ma'am," I said politely. "There are two kinds. I suspect you saw yours in India."

"Indeed I did."

"That was what they call here the *flamboyant*. The one over there has the same name, but it is the African tulip tree."

She nodded acceptance of this arboreal fact, and when my drink came I knocked it down straight again. Sat leaning back on one elbow and rattling the ice cubes around in the glass. The stately black gentleman entered the water with his dark wife and children, and they disported themselves near us with splashing glee.

I watched them with admiration. Phase Three was almost on us. When I did not erupt again, the hum of conversation arose and was almost back to normal when I twisted toward the old English woman on one elbow.

"Isn't that a happy-looking group?" I inquired. "Reminds me of a Georgia baptism. If they only had a couple of watermelons, we'd have a happy bunch of niggers there . . ."

My tone had been pitched conversationally, but perhaps a trifle high. The decibel count around the pool fell off to nothing, and the dignified black man bathing with his brood looked angrily toward me. He started wading toward the ladder, and his wife, her dark face concerned under the bathing cap of purple rubber flowers, put her hand on his arm. He shook it off and began climbing out of the pool.

Without warning, a young Negro man in a business

suit materialized at my side, and said that Mr. Rupert
Davies-Bishop, who was a prominent Antigua doctor,
had been offended by my conversation. Would I take
more care, please?

"Why?" I asked lazily. "Is he the head nigger around
here?"

Even the old English lady clucked at that. Davies-
Bishop came out of the pool like leviathan deserting
the deep, strode by me, and in passing jerked the little
metal table out from under my cigarettes and other
impedimenta. He had taken four more steps before I
lunged up and put him back in the pool.

A violent ballet then developed. The waiters con-
verged en masse, and one by one, I slipped their outstretched hands and flipped them into the water, hoping the poor bastards could swim. One of the yachtsmen, an enormous, shaggy-haired type, felt civil-
minded, and him I faked out of his faded tennis shoes,
kicked him in the crotch, butted him under the chin,
and heaved him in to join the others.

Several of them were now trying to get back out of
the pool and at me again, so I ran along its edge stamp-
ing on their fingers and kicking them in the face. It
was hard work at the shallow end, where they could
stand up, but easier in deep water. In the middle of
this gavotte, the white man in the business suit who
had been watching from the lobby materialized at my
elbow as I whirled. He began to admonish me loudly
so I grabbed the front of his chic tropic coat and
whirled him into the water.

When I had gone on another hand-stomping expedi-
tion, I was warned by a shrill cry of warning from the
old English lady. I turned to face a contingent from
the kitchen, three blacks, one with a meat cleaver. He
swung it with deadly intent, too, but I danced out of
range, butted him into the water, and cuffed his as-

sistants in beside him. Three of the thieving cab drivers came charging across the lobby, and I was delighted to see that one of them was the lout who had cheated me last night.

His face was contorted with fury, so I relaxed and spread my hands in supplication. The force of his charge carried him straight into me, so I sidestepped and put a vicious whip-block on him. The next two got straight gut punches, and one of them fell to his knees and began to vomit. The other one was still flailing away, so I yanked him around and punted him into the pool so hard I thought my foot was broken.

That done, I surveyed the pool again. The shaggy-haired yachtsman, having done his bit for racial equality, was getting out on the other side. His wife was shouting at him from the shade of the colonnaded table. The rest of them were standing in the pool staring at me, some in swimming trunks and others in saturated clothes. One of the angry waiters tried to crawl out of the side near me, so I stamped on his fingers and kicked him in the face.

When I went back to put on my stylish blue terry cloth jacket, and load its pockets with my cigarettes, lighter, and holder, the ancient English woman nodded with satisfaction.

"Good show," she said. "But I imagine the constabulary will be here soon."

"I expect so," I answered, and went back to my room.

The Honorable George

Faversham was presiding over the assizes in Georgetown, and I was hustled before him with dispatch by my private entourage of five black policemen. His Honor was an ample man the color of light coffee; his clean-cut features marked him nearly white. Clearly astonished, but maintaining his judicial mien, he stared down at me thoughtfully while the imposing list of charges was being read. When they were done, he leaned forward in his dark heavy-sleeved gown and addressed me.

"Sir, you seem to have created a scandal at Marmora Beach."

"That I did, Judge," I answered.

"Do you wish to make any statement in mitigation of your conduct, before I pass sentence upon you?"

"No, sir."

"You have nothing to say?"

"Only that I regret not having had more time. If I had, I'd have put the rest of those boyos in the pool."

"I see." The dark eyes were fixed on me. "It is the judgment of this court that you be fined $200 Eastern Currency, and that you secure passage out of Antigua on the *Federal Palm,* departing this afternoon. Corporal!"

"Sah!" The black policeman at my right snapped to attention.

"You and your men will escort Mr. Miles to Bennett's and wait while he procures a ticket on the *Palm.* You will then put him aboard the ship with his luggage. He is under deportation orders. And please inform Captain Agostini that he is to remain in his cabin, under guard, until the ship has cleared Antigua. Understood?"

"Sah!" The corporal nodded, and the judge rose to leave the bench.

"Your Honor," I called, and he turned and stood looking down at me. "Would it be possible for me to stop off at a general store for a few minutes on the way to the ship?"

"Yes. But I warn you, Mr. Miles, that if you have any further altercations, on the streets or aboard the ship, I will sentence you to a year in jail." He smiled slightly. "I don't think you would be temperamentally suited to our prison, so please do not erupt again in Antigua."

I nodded, and he swept out to his bare chambers, the hem of the heavy robe swinging. *A man of considerable dignity,* I thought as I signed a $100 traveler's check and gave it to his bailiff. When I went back out on the street, the sunlight hit me like a blow. The corporal strode along beside me until we came to Bennett's Travel Agency. There I bought a one-way passage to St. Sauteurs and nearly got into another hassle with the manager, who insisted that I must also buy a ticket from St. Sauteurs to the United States.

I explained to him that the law might require that I buy a continuing ticket from there, but that it was ridiculous that I be forced to buy a ticket returning me to my own country. The manager was pompous in his insistence, and I controlled my wrath by remembering Judge Faversham. So I wound up paying another $66 for a Liat Airline ticket from St. Sauteurs to St. Croix, in the American Virgins.

My police escort stood waiting while I shopped in a barnlike store for two bottles of Cutty Sark, two more of Mount Gay rum, some limes, and tinned biscuits. Our procession down the wharf to the gangplank of the *Federal Palm* was augmented by a pack of small black urchins who solicited me for various legitimate and immoral projects.

The *Palm* was a small cruise ship with a single blue funnel on her flying deck, and she was showing the corrosion of working tropic waters. The chief purser was a small, nearly white fellow, with a froggish face and the urbanity most such officers have when they deal with passengers. As he prepared to make out the ticket, I said that I wanted single occupancy of the cabin. He nodded and said that would be fifty percent more. While he was filling out the ticket, the police corporal stepped up beside me and repeated Judge Faversham's orders about my being confined to my cabin until the ship had cleared.

"Oh?" For the first time, the chief purser actually saw me. *A malcontent, eh?* he was thinking. There was a smaller desk beyond his, but no assistant purser was in sight. His superior handed me the impressive ticket, made change for my traveler's checks, and, stepping out into the companionway, called "Miss Ramjohn, please!"

A tall girl of principally East Indian ancestry came out of one of the cabins down the line and walked toward us. She was in her twenties, had classic features, long black hair, and the symmetry of a temple dancer just past ripeness. Her skin was ivory, with a hint of Negro blood. She said good morning to me and stood listening as the purser explained about my confinement. Further, that she was to do the guarding because his men were too busy for such nonsense.

". . . and I'm sure," he concluded, "that Mr. Miles has no mischief in mind. Had trouble here, did you, sir?"

"A fight," I explained, and he nodded and waved the police escort toward the gangplank. "Good show," the purser went on, "I hope you bashed them about properly."

"Had several in the air for a while," I admitted, and he laughed and left me in custody of Miss Ramjohn. I followed her down to my cabin, much admiring her undulations, and supervised the stowing of my luggage and parcels when they were brought along by two black seamen.

The cabin was small, but well-appointed; its air conditioning conduit was pouring cool air over the two bunks, high and low, and the one chair, mirror, and lavatory. When the seamen had withdrawn, Miss Ramjohn closed the cabin door and stood with her back to it, facing me. She smelled clean, with a faint fragrance of gardenias, and I was aware of the full breasts barely contained by her low-necked white blouse.

"Look," I said, washing my face and hands and looking at her in the mirror, "I'm not a murderer, Miss Ramjohn. Or at least not an Antiguan murderer, and I'll sit here in my own private chair quiet as a mouse until we're at sea. Deal?"

"I'm sorry, sir," said the tall girl. "My surveillance

is a condition of your passage, you see. I must follow
orders."

"All right. So be it. But I'm not going to let my life
be altered by your presence. Will you take the chair?"

"No, I'm quite comfortable," the Eurasian girl said,
so I shucked off my shirt, stepped out of my trousers,
and hung them up. Miss Ramjohn stared at the top
of the bulkhead closet and did not change expression.
Using a glass from the little cabinet and tap water, I
had a drink of rum and offered her one. She refused
gracefully, saying that she did not drink or smoke.
After clucking my sympathy at this state of affairs, I
had another drink, stretched out on the lower bunk,
and surveyed her.

"What's your first name?" I inquired. "I mean, after
all, two people who are this close . . . I can't call you
Miss Ramjohn all the way to St. Sauteurs."

"Clarrie," she said. The dark eyes flickered down
over me, recumbent on the bunk and wearing only
jockey shorts.

"Nobody's named Clarrie."

"For Claribelle."

Outside in the blasting heat of the wharf, winches
were rattling and whining, lowering pallets of cargo
into the aft hold. I could hear the humming of yellow
Hyster forklift trucks, and the chanting and cursing of
the stevedores. For twenty minutes I watched Clarrie
and she stared over my head. Finally, I decided I might
never get another chance of exactly this kind so I swung
my bare legs out of the bunk. Had another drink, and
taking Clarrie by both shoulders, kissed her. Gently and
insistently. Her skin was cool; the gardenia fragrance
stronger.

She made no gesture to push me away, nor did she
assist. She endured the caress pressed against the door.
I released her and stepped back.

"Where are you from?" I asked.

"Trinidad," she replied.

"Oh? That's the jump-up land, isn't it?"

For the first time she smiled. It wasn't much, but she had at least reacted, so I took her blouse off. The dark eyes swept down, startled, as I freed the three pearl buttons and drew the blouse down her arms. She wore no brassiere; had no need for any, because her dark-nippled breasts were perfectly shaped.

Her head had lifted again. When I began to kiss her breasts the aroused nipples hardened. I was watching her face; she shifted slightly on her feet, and the full mouth quivered. While I worked on her, silently, hurrying feet and fading voices passed along the companionway outside. When her breathing quickened, I unzipped the short skirt, let it fall, and worked her over down below.

This time, when I kissed her mouth again, the ivory hands with the dark nails tightened on my neck and drew me to her. We stood clasped together, and I ran my hands down the sweet curve of her flanks. She moaned, grinding against me, and I eased her around and into the bottom bunk. Stretched out there, with the glistening black hair fanned across the pillow, she was every man's dream of a wanton.

I had her three times in driving silence, and we were resting wordlessly when someone tapped on the cabin door. Called her name. Rising to one elbow, my dusky captor said in a high, clear English accent that everything was fine. *That she'd be along directly . . .*

I doubted that, and it turned out I was right.

If the preceding events

seem to you footling employment for a grown man, I'm not sure you'd be wrong. But it is what I do, and have done for fifteen years. My real name is Joseph Liam Gall and I am a counterintelligence agent, operating on individual contract for the action division of a large U.S. agency. In short, I am a nullifier, a minor strong-arm on the outermost periphery of American policy.

Looking back over my antic and often violent progress through the past decade and a half, I cannot truthfully say that my actions have affected history for very long, but like a good relief pitcher I have sometimes bought a little time for our more august representatives. I am highly paid, hold the hidden rank and perks of a Marine brigadier general (having been an officer in that service in War Two and Korea), and when not on assignment live in a huge clapboard castle in the Ozarks.

I restored the rococo mansion myself, and installed a greenhouse, mushroom culture room, and dojo gym in the basement. On the west slope I had dammed a thirty-foot icy waterfall to create a small lagoon, bordered by an Edo period Japanese garden complete with teahouse and a grotto; inside it I had built a sauna hut. The whole hilltop of my secluded estate was covered by a tall stand of virgin pines, and wind, rain, and snow harped through them in season. Until recently, there had also been three white tigers roaming my hundred-odd, high-fenced acres.

I had bought these unusual animals from the Maharaja of Rewa, who had bred the blue-eyed beasts to a true type, and when shipping them he had sent a *shikari,* or hunter, along to instruct me in their care. One of my principal joys had been watching the three snowy carnivores feed by moonlight in my garden, before the black bamboos, on horsemeat I had set out for them. So far as I knew, the Washington, D.C., Zoo had the only others in the United States.

Even Eden can be blasted. On my most recent assignment before this one in the Caribbean, I had gone undercover to infiltrate the most dangerous Black Power movement in the country. *The Republic of New Africa.* This group was a well-financed guerrilla army operating seventeen training cadres in the American South. They were buying land in counties which had a predominantly Negro population, raiding National Guard armories, and dispatching assassination squads to dispatch white bigots.

With my skin darkened by chemicals and wearing an Afro soul-brother wig, I got myself sentenced to a term in Arkansas's notorious Tucker Farm prison. Escaped from there with black inmate help, and got a job training black troopers at a major guerrilla installation at the edge of the Okefenokee Swamp in southern Georgia. While I was there, I went on two trips with the killer squads and was highly rated by Ahmed 4, the commander of the hidden camp.

Ahmed 4 was a tall man with ivory skin and the bearing of an Ashanti prince. He was completely dedicated to his dream of black supremacy, not equality, and he remains one of the few men I have feared in my lifetime. I was only a heartbeat away from death when he found out I was a plant, and had he not thought I could provide information, he would have killed me on the spot.

I broke out of his barracks lockup, and in crossing the eerie swamp blew up his communications powerhouse. He sent a squad of his troopers to attack my Ozark retreat, and I was driven from the house and took refuge in the cavern behind the waterfall. There had been a girl visiting me, a lady lawyer from Houston, dispatched from a major firm there to offer me a job, and she was killed.

The wooden mansion had been riddled by machine gun fire, and was partially burned. I had escaped, but was wounded, and four days later had been found wandering in the woods several miles away. Incoherent and dazed, with septicemia setting in as a result of abdominal gunshot wounds. I was lucky it was not peritonitis. After several months in Bethesda's Naval Hospital, outside Washington, I was released as fit.

Back home, I employed a construction firm in Springfield, Missouri, to repair the bullet and fire damage to the Ozarks hilltop house. To renovate the fourteen-foot ceilings and stained glass windows, and replace the charred rosewood panels. That job would take several months, and my contract in the hot islands of the lower Caribbean would use up most of that time.

Upon closer inspection,

the *Federal Palm* turned out to be even more of a rust bucket than I had first thought. After we had cleared St. John's harbor, Miss Ramjohn dressed and went about her other chores, cool and unruffled, and I toured the ship. Her brightwork was unpolished, her lifeboat frames rusting, and it was obvious that she was only an undistinguished ferryboat, coasting north from Trinidad to Jamaica, and back again. Passing her sister ship, the *Federal Maple,* en route. None of her ports was very far away, so she tied up most of every day and cleared just before dark.

The other passengers, from what I could see of them, seemed in perfect harmony with the run-down vessel. They were mostly elderly, retired people from the States or Canada, with about 40 percent of them Negro or colored. These last were obviously people of some status in the islands, government servants or important business men. One couple I could not place; they were in their twenties, he was dark-haired and looked fit but not rugged, and she was a blonde with straight flaxen hair and pink skin. All over; the shapely legs projecting from the microskirt were almost shocking pink.

Aft on the small cruise ship, beyond the hatch and concealed from the main passenger deck, was a deck-passage dormitory, which amounted to fresh air steerage. In this area the dark peasantry were carted from island to island for about $1 a day, but had to furnish their own food and any other comforts. Deck cargo, empty pallets, bunches of live chickens and pigs, and clusters of fruit strewed the aft hatch, and no attempt was made to straighten the tangle while at sea.

After taking several turns around the main deck, and the upper promenade deck that held the three luxury suites and the captain's and chief engineer's quarters inside, and the lesser officers' quarters opening onto the deck, I tried to go up to the bridge deck, but was turned back by the watch officer. As I nodded and went back down the metal stairway, I could see the island of Montserrat looming ahead. In the late afternoon, patches of dark green shadow were drifting across its flanks, and a bending curtain of rain was torn from the clouds around its saw-toothed crest.

I stepped over the bulkhead into the air conditioning of the lower deck and returned to my cabin. Closed the door behind me and stood with my back to it, as Clarrie Ramjohn had done earlier. We had frolicked in the lower berth, but there was something different about the articles I had laid on the unused upper berth's surface. The airmail copy of *Newsweek* I had bought in Antigua was out of place; the little packet of limes had been moved.

I shook the bunk down carefully and found two sealed packages, pliofilm wrapped. They had been wedged back of the pillow, under the mattress, and hefting them I made their total weight at two kilos. Nearly four-and-a-half pounds. I locked the door behind me and broke the seal on one of the packages. Tasted its contents and grimaced.

The contraband which had been planted in my cabin was not marijuana, what they call "ganja" in these hot islands. It was considerably tougher than that. "Cannabis indica," hashish, the dried pistillate of the East Indian hemp plant now grown all over the world. It could be smoked, chewed, or taken in liquid, and, unlike ganja, would make you bark like a fox and run straight up the wall.

The ship's motion altered as she reversed for an anchorage outside Plymouth, capital of Montserrat, and I knew if the tip had gone out to the authorities there, and ey caught me with the coarse gray narcotic in my possession I would be jailed for some time. Perhaps even draw a long jail term after they talked with that judge in Antigua. Wrapping the two limp packages in my big beach towel, and throwing my bathing trunks and blue jacket over the other arm, I turned abruptly out of the cabin.

I did not go forward toward the salon and bar, but out the back door toward the aft deck, into the blistering heat of the hatch. Then up the starboard-side stairway to the promenade deck and along it forward, and down again into the air conditioning. I found the cabin of the assistant purser where I thought it would be, across the ship from the Purser's Office, and nobody was in the companionway when I stopped and fiddled the lock in about ten seconds.

Like all the other cabin doors, it opened with an ancient, tubular brass key, and you can beat such locks with a stout pipe cleaner. Assistant Purser John Ratoon was still not at home. A soiled white uniform was thrown across the bunk, another clean one was hanging in the wardrobe. I thrust the packages of hashish far back on the top shelf, stepped back out of the cabin, and relocked its door.

I got away with it only because all the action was on the other side of the deck, where the gangplank was clanking down and the passengers were bombarding the purser with questions. He kept answering patiently, a half-white, frog-faced little man, that we would be at Montserrat until eleven that night, but that passengers had to be back aboard by ten. Yes, the ship's launch would be making trips to the pier the whole time we were there . . .

They kept yapping at him. We would have two hours more of daylight ashore, he said; the stores and cafés were being kept open, because a ship's arrival was an event on Montserrat. I stood at the far edge of the badgering pack, and watched the customs, immigration, and police officials of Montserrat come aboard. They stepped off the top of the rickety gangplank, natty in white shorts, short-sleeved shirts, and black helmets, and the one with the most braid on his cap had a word with the frog-faced purser.

Listening, his face lifted to stare at me as if he had known where I was standing, he called Miss Ramjohn. She escorted the two police officers down the companionway to my cabin and unlocked it for them. I went into the bar off the dingy salon and had a straight Demerara rum, with iced soda and a nip of lime on the side. The launch left for Plymouth with the first load of cackling passengers, and after twenty minutes the police came into the bar and asked to see my passport, medical record, and continuing ticket out of the Caribbean Islands.

I showed them these things, including the ticket to St. Croix I had not wanted to buy. They thanked me politely and left the bar. Such interest in an in-transit passenger was unusual, and everybody on the ship knew it. When the launch came back, I rode into the Plymouth pier on it, after having glimpsed Miss Ramjohn staring at me from the companionway.

I walked along the ramshackle pier shaking off small black boys who wanted a handout. One ten-year-old, barefooted and kneeling on a bollard, asked me for a dollar. He did it offhandedly, a pure ebony wiseacre in rags, so I turned in the late afternoon heat and asked why he needed a dollar when everybody else was ready to settle for pennies.

"I'm studyin' to be a saga boy, mon," he answered easily. "Rest of these chaps tiefs and small boys."

"How saga boy?" I insisted.

"Oh, I got to buy beer and cigarettes, mebbe join up with steel band," he said. "You gonna gib me *my* dollah?"

"Never in this world," I answered.

The urchin's mouth registered sadness. "Boss," he said, "you've let me down . . ."

I laughed aloud, and his white teeth flashed. When I flipped him half a dollar, he drew it in as casually as Bill Russell taking a pass-off. I followed him into Plymouth, after refusing a guided tour that would cost several more "dollahs" and yield some unspeakable delights. The town was as nondescript in the late light as most of those at the edge of these lower, mountainous islands.

Walking down the main street, I passed the usual Canadian banks, Barclay's, the factors and shipping agent's offices, and looked into the fluorescent glare of "Lindy Eide," the New York store. There is one on nearly every island, and this one was owned by Abe Massief, a Syrian. And for an island with only fifteen thousand people on it, the emporium was a busy place.

Three checkout stands, National Cash Registers, moveable counters and turnstiles . . . Clothing section, whiskey and spirits department, groceries. I walked on until I came to the frame building with porches all around it, shaded by an enormous banyan tree. The Carnegie Library, usually the only well-run thing in the islands. I sauntered up on the porch, nodded to the intelligent-looking black girl back of the desk, and browsed along the shelves until I came to the back door. There I stepped out, went around the multi-rooted trunk of the tree with its spreading canopy, and waited.

Not long. A stocky, middle-aged man with a swarthy complexion joined me on the seaside of the huge tree.

"Abe Massief?"

"Yes. And you?"

I gave him the word, which was not my real name or my cover name, but the assignment name, and he nodded. While he was talking in a low voice only tinged with an English accent, I studied him. They say that the Syrians showed up in these islands long ago, with unvarying results. They got off the ships from the Levant so poor that they could only afford pushcarts, and hawked fruit and produce through the streets. Then, a year later they opened a hole-in-the-wall store, and in the second year, enlarged it.

These Syrians took no interest in politics, society, or sports. After the third year, they enlarged the store again and moved out of the humid, seaside towns up onto the slopes. In ten years, they had the best stores in town and the highest houses. I could believe it. This little man was reporting to me like a computer, and yet my agency had not placed him on Montserrat. But, for two decades now the agency had been paying him a monthly fee, in a Jamaican bank, to keep reporting as he prospered.

He did not know of any accumulation of arms on

Montserrat, he said. Unless it was the American Negro at Vue Point, who had last year opened a beach concession beside the hotel. He took parties spearfishing, water-skiing, and hunting. Had seven shotguns. But there was really nothing to hunt on the island, if you excepted agouti and the mongoose.

On the other hand, the local government was so inept that it could be taken over with seven shotguns. Or seven cricket bats in strong hands. No, there was no subversive party on the island, but the usual lot of ne'er-do-wells, getting drunk on rum, and occasionally rampaging with whistling cutlasses . . . He had heard no whisper of a plot to seize shipping or communications.

"Do you know John Ratoon?" I asked, and he nodded.

"The assistant purser on the *Palm*. Been making this port for nearly a year now. Has many friends here. Unusual to make so many friends so fast, for a Yank."

"Are you sure he's a Yank?"

"Certainly. I've talked with him many times in my stores."

The sun was lowering toward the western horizon; the island was beginning to darken. The blue water was leaden, catspawed by wavelets.

"Could you find out, quietly, if he is working on the ship this trip. I got on at Antigua, but I haven't seen him on board."

"Certainly." Massief turned and left me, walking toward the center of Plymouth, a great deal of which he owned. I sat down on one of the draping roots falling from the huge banyan tree, lighted a cigarette, and stared out over the sea. *No one had told me that John Ratoon was an American . . .*

The Syrian merchant was back in twenty minutes. "On the ship," he reported, "they say Ratoon was

brought low by malaria in Kingston, and did not sail
with them."

"Okay." I stood up.

"On the other hand," the Syrian continued, "the
black dwarf was on the Soufrière beach this afternoon."

"So?" I felt that I had missed a key sentence somewhere.

"Yes. Ratoon seems to use this little fellow from St.
Sauteurs, a black dwarf named Timothy George, as a
court jester. Timothy never travels on the *Palm* or
Maple, but often shows up in advance of Ratoon. I
suppose he moves about on interisland schooners or
sloops. Ratoon makes a great thing of him in the rum
shops."

"You mean," I inquired sharply, "that this Timothy
bypasses customs and immigration?"

"Oh, sir," said the Syrian, "half the economic life
of these islands stems from smuggling and illegal entry.
They have coast guard boats, but the crews are mostly
drunk or helping the smugglers. And who would bother
with Timothy George?"

"I see," I said. "Thank you, Mr. Massief."

"It is nothing," he said. "May I go now?"

"Yes, of course," I said, and he went back around
the banyan tree in his rubber Bata shoes, which cost
more on the islands than they did in the United States.
But not for Massief.

I waited twenty minutes and walked back through
the town to the pier. There, under shaded warehouse
lights, crates of limes and bales of sea-island cotton
were being loaded on lighters to be towed out to the
Federal Palm, which was now blazing with lights. The
ship's launch was nowhere in sight, and I could not
make out if it was at the *Palm's* side. So I struck a $4
Biwee deal for two oarsmen in a small boat to row me

to the ship, and as we approached her we could hear the winches whining, loading cargo off the lighters lined up at her starboard side.

There was almost no sea running, and as we approached the *Palm* my oarsmen pulled alongside her. I saw that they were passing too close to the winch area and shouted from my seat in the rear of their craft, but they laughed. It was dark in the lee of the *Palm,* and when they shipped oars and let us drift, we bumped into one of the loaded lighters.

The whining winch above us was lifting pallets of cargo loaded from the lighters by sweating black stevedores. I promised myself that the winch was moving within its circumscribed arcs, but then I glanced up and changed my mind. Instead of swinging the load inward over the hatch, the netted pallet swung out in a wide circle over our small boat.

Instinctively I went overboard, and a split-second later the few tons the pallet was carrying dropped and smashed the bottom out of the dinghy. As I surfaced in the dark water, I could see one of the oarsmen crushed, and had a fleeting picture of the other dark body eeling over the side before the stove-in craft disintegrated.

I swam to the bottom of the gangplank and heaved myself up on its rounded bottom. I had lost only my beach towel and a set of bathing trunks, but I knew one of the oarsmen was dead, and possibly, the other. There was no way the man handling the winch could have swung his pallet load that far out without premeditation.

When I got to the top of the gangplank, dripping, I had to force my way through a flock of gabbling passengers. I broke through them, and the bland purser followed me down the companionway to my cabin. He said he was very sorry: *such a stupid accident* . . .

I said yes, indeed, and if it kept up, it would give the line a bad name. Unlocked my cabin door and stalked into it, dripping sea water.

Half an hour later the

Montserrat police were back in my cabin. Or at least their chief was; the other two stood out in the companionway while he interrogated me. I told him nearly all that had happened, and he confirmed my opinion that one of the boatmen was dead with a smashed spine. He had caught the full force of the runaway cargo when it stove in the boat. The other had been struck only a glancing blow; he had both legs broken, but would survive.

When the chief had run out of questions, I gave him two $100 traveler's checks, saying that $150 of it was for the family of the dead man and the other $50 for the boatman in the hospital. He said that was handsome of me, saluted, and led his dark associates down the companionway toward the gangplank. He was still puzzled, and I didn't blame him. Before my arrival, he had been tipped that I was a hashish smuggler.

I had come up clean on that charge, yet an hour later I was the center of unexplained violence, in which two natives of this island had been involved. One was dead and the other badly hurt, while I didn't have a scratch on me. What I hadn't told him was why I had left the rowboat so precipitately. I had been sitting in its stern seat, swinging to the gentle chop of the harbor, when I had looked up toward the main deck and seen Clarrie Ramjohn staring down at me.

I had been about to wave when her fixed gaze changed to fright. Both hands flew up to her face involuntarily as she turned her head and looked directly at the shirtless black winch operator. His back was to me, but I noticed the pallet of cargo swing wildly out of its normal parabola. That was when I had gone knifing into the water.

The Eurasian girl had known the attempt on my life was coming, but had not thought I would be watching her. Putting on a tie and jacket, musing about my probable life expectancy aboard the *Federal Palm,* I went forward and down the steep steps into the dining salon. At first glance it seemed well ordered, but as I was shown to my place at a table for four the gim-crackery started becoming obvious.

The snowy napkins placed in the wine glasses were paper, and the glasses themselves were plastic. Although the *Federal Palm* moved from day to day between tropic islands where orchids, heliconia, ginger, and bird-of-paradise flowers grew like weeds, the blooms in the wall vases were Hong Kong-made and imperishable. I would not have caviled at such cheapness, except that the ship charged very handsome prices and could have afforded better.

Another couple was escorted to the table, and we nodded and introduced ourselves. They were Richard and Hazel Hughes, and she sat down in a whirl of knees and thighs below the miniskirted black linen dress. She was the pink girl with the good legs I had seen up on the promenade deck, and the spare, dark-browed man was her husband of eight months. Both were Welsh. He had his doctorate as a metallurgist, and for the past two years had been working as a professor at the University of British Columbia, in Vancouver.

Every once in a while, the blind hog finds an acorn; these were delightful people. Richard was twenty-nine, she two years younger, and her sister had married his twin brother. Richard shook his head sadly about Hazel's pinkness. He said that they had traveled in Mexico and Central America on his vacations, and that she *would* stay out in the sun. When she did, inevitably, she turned pink as a neon sign.

"Doesn't she blister?" I asked, laughing at his resigned air.

"Never. If she did that and suffered horribly, I could have my vengeance, you see. But no. Just turns pink like this, and when hazed into the shade, slowly turns pale again."

They had completed his teaching contract in Canada, and were taking this Jamaica-to-Trinidad cruise before returning to the United Kingdom, where he would be a professor at Leeds University, working mostly in metal research. Since he had said that he had two other degrees, Cambridge, with honors, I asked if he was not interested in teaching at one of our U.S. universities.

"Never," the dark Welshman stated emphatically.

"Why not? The money's good, isn't it?"

"Of course it is. Grand, the money. But they're a pack of bloody fools, those Yanks."

I laughed so hard I nearly upset my soup, which was onion and good. We were working on the sliver of fish, covered with a piquant sauce, but no more palatable for that because it was refrigerated, when our laughing intimacy came to a lurching halt. A tall Englishman in his late fifties was escorted to our table and took the place across from me.

He had a handsome, florid face, military bearing, and the ramping manner of the classic upper-class English homosexual. His name, we were privileged to learn, was Peter Frampton. The way he supplied the first name, it came out "Petah." He wore a well-cut but shabby bush jacket with a bright yellow ascot, and tufts of wild white hairs projected from his ears and nostrils.

While he was waiting for his soup, I remarked on the bush jacket, and he glanced at me but did not reply at once. Snapped his fingers and ordered the maitre d' to have him sent down, from the bar, a double rum on the rocks. *Cockade brand, Barbados, please!* Then he turned his attention back to me and said that the bush jackets were made up for him in London.

"Sentiment, really, I suppose. I'm a retired colonel; led the West African Rifles in Burma, matter of fact. But quite suitable to this climate too, don't you think?"

I said I thought so. Richard and Hazel Hughes had turned silent, so I had to assume the conversational role with him. I knew, but did not tell him I knew, that the West African Rifles had gotten the shit kicked out of them in the Salween Valley, because I had been running an airport north of there. In Dinjan, Upper Assam, India. Our flights ran from Calcutta to Assam and across the Himalayas to wartime China, and many of my pilots had flown over the scenes of his unit's agony in the jungles.

Colonel Frampton, retired, took over our table as though it was privileged to be hearing the anecdotes he had dined out on in London long ago. *Sweet Jesus,* I thought, *it's been thirty years, Colonel. We have new wars, new problems. You're maundering . . .*

Petah was not dismayed. When his glass of dark

rum came, he knocked it off in one, like a medicinal draught, and attacked his soup between stories, comments, and antic persiflage. He reminded the silent Welshman, after hearing that he and the pink girl had been so shortly married, that what had been idle fornication before would now be adultery. He told the story about Mrs. Patrick Campbell and the New York cab driver, after her Pekingese had crapped in the back seat. The cabbie had objected bitterly, and Mrs. Campbell fixed him with an imperious eye. "Young man!" she ordered briskly, "you are not to abuse the dog. *I* did it. Please present your bill to the desk." And she sailed on into the Waldorf lobby.

His compulsive act as *raconteur* was like the buzzing of moths around our ears. Then, without warning, he decided to get current and began discussing the Black Power activities in Trinidad and Jamaica. His high voice carried well, unfortunately, and nearly half the hundred passengers dining in the plastic salon were Negro or colored.

"Stupid bahstards!" he pronounced. "They burn banks, invade schools, incite to riot . . . What would they replace it with, the system we left? Nothing. Mindless buggers, that's what they are, not a brain cell working . . ."

The Welsh couple and I were by now having cheese, crackers, and excellent coffee. Our heads were down, but those of the other diners were turning toward the tirade. Even the seemingly disinterested waiters, all Negro on this all-Negro-owned-and-operated cruise ship, were listening.

"Left them, don't y'know, a civil service system better than the world ever knew before," continued the florid colonel. His ascot was coming askew because of his fulsome gestures. "Left them a judicial system not matched anywhere in the world, not even in your country, Yank, although it's based on ours."

"Not in Louisiana," I said. "Common law there based on the Napoleonic Code."

"Right, but generally. I have many friends among the planters, y'know. The ones who have stayed and are trying to tough it out, and those who've given up and gone back to the U.K. Do you know what they think the principal trouble is?"

"No."

"The sodding breadfruit tree. The beggars can have one or two on their small holdings, so they sleep on their lazy arses all day, occasionally plucking a breadfruit from the tree. No way, you see, to get a day's honest work out of them."

"Then you lament the passing of slavery?" I asked in innocence, and Hazel Hughes stuffed her paper napkin in her mouth to keep from laughing out loud.

"A typically stupid Yank remark," stated Colonel Frampton. "You're thinking in terms of monkeys straight out of the tree, like Stokely Carmichael, who by the by is barred for life from his native Trinidad. The people in many of these islands have been free for a hundred years or more."

So saying, he attacked his mixed grill with relish. I glanced at Richard Hughes, fluttered my eyelids to ask forgiveness, and got up.

"I'll say goodnight now. Mrs. Hughes, Richard, Colonel . . ."

The colonel stabbed a fork at me. "Remember, it was the breadfruit did it. Far worse than the dole."

"Yes, sir," I said, and walked toward the steep stairway, aware of the hostile regard of the waiters and most of the diners. I went to my cabin, searched it thoroughly again, and took off my tie and jacket. Then I went up to the promenade deck and watched Plymouth's cluster of lights recede. The moon was out, silvering the wavelets of the Caribbean. Low, scudding clouds made fantastic shadows on the heaving plain of water. The sea on the Atlantic side of these islands is far more severe; its waves crash on the beaches like freight trains, and have rocks whirling in their undertow.

Passengers kept coming up the stairs, hurrying to get preferred positions in the thicket of folding chairs, which had sprung up on the aft deck. There was to be a movie; several, in fact. I had seen the notice posted on the ship's bulletin board. Two ancient American westerns, Grade B, and a documentary on Trinidad's power generator facilities. I was not beguiled by the possibilities and moved to the starboard rail. From there, still distant but brooding under a dark, motionless cloud, Dominica loomed ahead.

A rapid step sounded behind me and I whirled. But it was only Colonel Frampton coming toward me in the moonlight. He had removed the ascot and gotten another glass of straight rum. Sighing, he lounged beside me, elbows on the salt-encrusted rail.

"That's the wild island," he said. "Always has been. And y'know, when you pronounce its name properly, *Domineeka,* in the States or U.K., almost everybody will think you're referring to the Dominican Republic, where that bloody mulatto, Trujillo, was supported so long by your government."

I said that I knew the Dominican Republic shared the island of Hispaniola with Haiti, and that our Marines had been in *there* for donkey's years.

He nodded. "Collecting the *douane* and taxes, weren't they, to pay off a New York bank?"

"I think that was the position, yes."

He was silent for a moment. "That Papa Doc Duvalier in Haiti's another bleeding sweetheart. Understand the old pickney sits in his bathtub in a top hat, practicing *obeah.*"

The Englishman was such a parody of a Noel Coward character that I was getting irritated with him. "Colonel," I asked, "if conditions in these black island republics, or whatever they are, upset you so much why don't you get out of them?"

He took a long slug of his iced rum. "Can't, you know. Own a small house outside Montego Bay in Jamaica, and that defines my fortunes. Make a few quid doing historical articles for journals nobody reads, but cannot, of course, live on that and my mil'try retirement pay in England."

I didn't answer, and it was just as well. If I had, I would have said that he probably augmented his standard of living, such as it was, by spending fortnights with friends in Barbados and the other islands, until by inevitable attrition of his ancient anecdotes they ceased to be friends.

"Look," he said hesitantly, "I realize that you and the Welsh couple thought me a bit vociferous at table. And I am damned rude, I know. But y'see, I belonged to a class that had everything. Manners, courage, style if you like. And it was wiped out almost overnight."

"I understand. But the fundamental is that you were the burra sahibs all over the world, at someone else's expense. And when the millions of dark people you were exploiting began to shrug their shoulders and lift their heads in question, you had to be thrown off their backs. They may make complete balls of their own destinies, but now, at least, they are in charge of them."

"I expect you're right," said Colonel Frampton mildly. It was the first comment I had heard him make without heat, emphasis, or rancor. "Just the same, it was a golden time . . ."

"Do you know Evelyn Waugh's *Handful of Dust,* the novella?" I asked.

"Quite well," he said quietly.

"There's a line in it that sums up what you're talking about. The lord of the manor's wife has taken up with a bad hat named Beaver, you remember, and at his club he talks to his wife on the phone. She says that she is going to live with Beaver, and makes some impossible demands. The gentleman husband agrees and hangs up the phone, realizing that he will have to sell the manor house and break up the estate."

"Right. I remember."

"Then Mr. Waugh comments: 'The cream and dappled unicorn had fled the forest glade; a whole Gothic age had come to grief . . .'"

We both watched the dark cloud ahead in its almost permanent position. Shrouding the summit of Mount Diablotin on Dominica. The slaty Caribbean Sea creamed by the sides of the ship and went rushing back to join the foaming wake.

"That about says it," agreed Colonel Frampton. "Good night, sir." Rattling the ice in his glass, he moved away briskly. *To drink in the bar,* I reflected, *hoping Camelot would return.* Going to his cabin at eleven, when it closed . . . The cabin which he probably shared with a polite dark man.

When the movie started, its dialogue distorted by the sea breeze whipping past the amplifiers, I moved to the main deck and checked the purser's cabin. Open, but no one there. Then I went up to the bridge, and this time no one challenged me. Up on the deserted flying bridge, supposedly closed to passengers, I took up my vigil. I was sitting on the crosspiece of a lifeboat's A-frame, watching the door of John Ratoon's cabin. There was no light in it. Time passed.

Occasionally I could hear faint snatches of wind-blown dialogue from the movie or audience response. From where I was sitting, Dominica's dark bulk, with its overhanging cloud, was also in my line of vision, and I reviewed what I knew about the place. For one thing, the taxi ride from its airport (the landing strip short, dangerous, and ending in the sea) to Roseau, the capital, was the longest in the world. About forty miles through lush valleys, high fern forests, and wild tropic jungles. These jungles were shaded by gommier and ceiba trees more than a hundred feet high, and there was a cathedral hush in their sunless aisles.

The only sound to be heard there was the plaintive cry of the "siffleur de montaigne," a rare whistling bird found nowhere else. The rainfall in the mountainous interior was measured in feet, not inches, and the island had over three hundred rivers. A sulfurous boiling lake was high in its center and could be reached only by a three-hour climb. The area around it looked like a lunar landscape seen in a dream.

Dominica was called the baleful island, the refuge of misfits and eccentrics. Here, slowly being eroded by miscegenation and the heart-bursting consumption of raw white rum, were the last remnants of the Carib Indians. With only a few-score pure specimens remaining on a reservation near Salybia, these fierce warriors were slowly dying out.

They had been the kings of creation in their time. A century before the Spaniards, French, and English had arrived, these copper-colored people with long, glossy black hair, clean-cut features, and Mongolian cheekbones had come north in their long canoes. From the Orinoco River basin, most authorities said. I had seen the few pure Carib remnants, and they looked much like the Mayans in Yucatan to me. They were cruel, cannibalistic, and easily overwhelmed the gentle Arawak Indians who had inhabited the Caribbean Islands. Eating the men, keeping the women for procreation, and speaking three languages.

One was a corruption of the Arawak tongue, to speak with the women and children; another was straight Carib for ordinary talk; and the third dealt with war plans. Anticipating chemical warfare, these Caribs used clouds of hot-pepper smoke to drive away invaders. Driven to bay, finally, in Dominica, located between the French islands of Guadeloupe and Martinique, they made this island the last one conquered by European invaders.

Because of its steepness and the inaccessibility of most of its surface, Dominica escaped the usual exploitation for a long time. Prince Rupert's Bay, its one fine natural harbor, was for years a mouldering ruin because of endemic yellow fever and malaria, and the town there, Portsmouth, remained only a village. The capital was established at Roseau, which is a dismal, sunbaked place with no harbor at all, and only a ramshackle pier for small craft.

Because of these facts, Dominica has known some of the strangest expatriates in history. After World War One, two British officers, retired, bought a small plantation and decided to get their dark servants cracking. They drilled them by moonlight, after the normal work day, shouting close-order drill instructions at their shambling blacks until they were forced off the island by their mutinous troops.

A young, handsome Englishman once got off a freighter, waved it goodbye, and bought a small plantation. Lime trees; this island has the largest lime groves in the world. They supply the famous English firm, Rose's, with most of its basic juices. The newcomer turned out to be rich, but he neglected his lime orchards. Instead, he put in a full day, every day, digging a large hole. By himself. It was later determined that his young wife had died in Australia, and that he was creating a corridor to rejoin her.

An American gentleman, also wealthy, came here and became even more affluent. He was the last hop-skip-and-jump Olympic champion in the world. The last because shortly after he won the title, the event was dropped from competition. He became a fierce and brawling member of Dominican society, and is well remembered.

A German Jew from Liverpool dropped off a freighter one day, opened a small store in Roseau, and in a few years was known as "La Falaise," ("the cliff which causes the downfall of the ladies"). He set up a chain of stores, some in the most remote hamlets, and in each one his manager and mistress was the prettiest girl in town. He was on the road most of the time.

Another English eccentric was called by the natives "Captain Welcome," because he always fired his shotgun, without warning, at any interloper on his plantation grounds.

After I had kept my vigil for over three hours, watching the entrance to Ratoon's cabin, I decided that the assistant purser was either not on the ship or was bunking somewhere else. I was standing up, stretching and preparing to go below from my windy eyrie, when someone came up from the main deck and mounted the ladder to the bridge deck. The movies had been over for an hour, and I watched the indistinct figure move below me.

It stopped back of the lighted wheelhouse, and I went down the iron steps swiftly. When the key grated in the lock of the radio shack and the lights inside were flipped on, I had a good look at the nocturnal prowler. It was Thomas, the handsome, slightly fat bar-boy, who had impressed me mostly, before, with his indolence.

He was not indolent now. The door swung closed behind him and was locked from the inside. I heard him flipping switches. A low hum penetrated through the door of the wireless shack. Thomas cleared the key, rattling away with a practiced fist, and began sending in CW far faster than I could follow.

I ran toward the iron stairway, dropped down two decks, and opened the bulkhead door into the air-conditioned coolness of the main passenger deck. In my cabin, I loaded the tiny German recorder, and went back through the deserted companionway and up the flights of metal stairs.

He was still sending, rattling the key too fast for me to read. I switched on the recorder and held it at the crack of the locked door. The clacking could have been taped from farther than that. He continued sending for another ten minutes, cleared his key again, and through his amplifier I could hear answering clicks. The switches were cut, but before he opened the door I had faded away, walking forward on my rubber-soled shoes.

Down in my cabin, I turned the volume low and re-played the telegraphic messages at slow speed. Because I was unfamiliar with the code, I had to run them through several times. But the message was clear, and had been sent in the clear. This meant that they were stupid, or contemptuous of my ability to eavesdrop on them.

What the message said (and I suspected that it had been sent at reduced power, to be receivable only on Dominica) was interesting.

ATTEMPT ON GALL FAILED IN MONTSERRAT. IMPERATIVE SAME MISTAKE NOT BE MADE DOMINICA. HE IS BIG C FROM WASHINGTON'S D.C. MAN. WHOLE PROJECT IN JEOPARDY.

DO NOT UNDERESTIMATE. HE SUCCESSFULLY
SWITCHED H PLANT TO R'S CABIN.

The message, before sign-off, had been ended with
only "T." Pretty cute, I thought; the bastard phrases
like a pro. And they've known my name all the time.
My real name.

I sat on the edge of the lower bunk, hands swinging
from the motion of the boat. At some point in every
operation, there comes a time when my notoriety in
the spook trade becomes a problem. Because I had
worked for so many years all around the world, there
were some places where my very presence precluded
any success. I was known as a nullifier, a stopper,
whose rental of a hotel room would cause around-the-
clock surveillance.

So I wondered if I was too exposed on this one. And
decided to let it ride until I had talked to the Dominican
contact. He had been highly recommended, and if he
said nay, the agency could pull somebody in from Trinidad or Barbados . . . Wedging the chair under the
brass doorknob, I had a drink of warm rum and
flopped on the lower bunk. Ordering myself to awaken
in three hours, just before dawn.

Before I dropped off, I remembered something else
about the Carib Indians. Something relevant. When
undertaking a war journey in their long canoes, it was
their custom to adopt a pseudonym, so that all actions
during their absence could be considered as done by
unknown strangers.

That summed me up pretty well, so I fell into a
troubled sleep.

I went ashore the next

morning before breakfast. A local launch bearing fresh fruits and vegetables came out to the *Palm* from Roseau, so I swung aboard when it started back. The sun was just clearing the towering bulk of Dominica, lightening its steep green flanks, and the forbidding cloud was still hovering over Mount Diablotin, concealing its crest. The stores in Roseau were not open yet, and I walked southeastward through the crooked streets.

I passed a closed office with a blue, circular sign on the front door. "DOMINICA SAFARIS" read the legend on the sign, and in its center was a green palm tree. Parked in a neat row before the office were four custom-made Land Rovers with removable tops; they all held the same insignia. The Liat Airways office was next, also closed, and as I went up the road I passed the Fort Young Hotel, with its ancient cannons flanking the lobby entrance.

Another quarter of a mile and I was passing the stone gates leading to the Botanical Gardens, which are among the finest in the world. The inevitable cricket pitch was just beyond that, and I paced across the grass to the wooden tier of seats, empty now except for a tall man with shaggy hair down to his shoulders. The hair had been bleached flaxen by the Dominican sun, and the Nordic-looking face was tanned mahogany.

He nodded, and I sat down beside him and lighted a little cigar. When I asked if he was Ian Mackenzie, he said, "That's right."

"I'm off the *Palm*," I said, and he said he knew, that he had been expecting me. Mackenzie was thirty years old, had been a merchant seaman, yachtsman, U.S. Marine, and for the past four years he and his London partner had operated Dominica Safaris, training guides to operate the special Land Rovers. So much of the island could not be reached by roads that their smartly planned operation drew large parties from the few cruise boats that stopped at the island.

"I don't know how much you know about this deal," I continued, "but I think I'm in trouble. And it's about to get worse."

"I don't know much. I just follow the orders your people send down."

Partially, I revealed the rumored take-over of transportation and communications in the islands, and Mackenzie whistled in astonishment. He asked what the dumb bastards hoped to gain by such a take-over, since if it was only partly successful they would become responsible for the lives of thousands of U.S., British, and Canadian nationals.

"Every front page in the world, for one thing," I answered.

"Certainly. But where will they hide after it's done? Not on these hot islands. Even if they grab a few governments, what will they do with them?"

I shrugged. "What about this opposition Freedom Party here? Can it win at the polls? Could it seize the government here by force?"

Mackenzie stared at the toes of his polished boots. "Never win an election," he stated. "Labor's been in for ten years here, and this Freedom Party sounds revolutionary with its campaigning, but it's mostly financed by the white planters. No, they might have cached some arms; you could smuggle elephants into this place . . ."

I told him about the hashish plant in my cabin, and the attempt on my life. Did he know John Ratoon?

"Seen him, is all. Popular here, with the strong-arm boys. Plays rough. Could be a connection, I suppose." He fell silent, and I waited. "Three years ago, the Dominican government deported five American Negroes. They had planted a whole plantation in ganja on the other side of the island. But I think they were from Detroit . . ."

I asked him about the standby racing yacht that the agency had chartered for me. It was to await my instructions while standing off Dominica in international waters. My contact was to be through Mackenzie's Safari offices. He monitored several frequencies on his receivers, and had a transmitter. In the event I chose not to call the yacht in, it had been ordered to trail the *Palm* down the islands until, and if, I needed it.

"You're in luck there," said Ian. "*Romany Two* called in late yesterday afternoon, and she's a sparkling marvel. A hundred-tonner, ninety-one feet overall, a masthead yawl-rigged beauty. For auxiliary power, twin 671 General Motors diesels, 225 horses each.

Black-hulled, and her big fore-triangle makes her hell on wheels going to weather . . ."

He shook his head admiringly, and I remarked that the two of them ought to get married. He grinned sheepishly, and I decided he would be a good man in a hard spot.

"Like to have her," he admitted. "She's based in St. Sauteurs and owned by Carl Stock. Normally, he skippers her on charter, too."

"Normally?"

"Broke his leg last month. Probably loaded; he's a fair jug baby. On your charter she's skippered by his sister, Martha."

"His *sister*, for Christ's sake! What kind of a lash-up is this? Man, I'm on urgent business, maybe in a bind, and what I don't need is somebody's baby sister—"

"Peace!" Ian held up both weathered hands. "Wait until you see her. She's a big blond bird, thirtyish, tall as you are and much better built. Twice-married, and as capable with deep-sea racing yachts as anybody in the Caribbean. Two years ago, brought a single-hander from the Canaries to Barbados, on the nose. Has crewed for Carl in most of the international races, and they've won their share."

"Who crews for her, while Carl has broken legs?"

"Three black boys from St. Sauteurs. Don't worry about her. She'll get you where you want to go and not ask questions. At the price you're paying, she's got no right to ask questions."

"Okay, I'll pass it for the time being. What kind of communications equipment has *Romany* got?"

"The best in the world, for something her size. A 400-watt single side-band with thirty channels. That means sixty crystals, to send and receive, and from here you can work New York or London direct on it."

I nodded and got up. "Tell Miss Stock to keep

standing off, and I'll advise her what to do next, before going back aboard the *Palm*."

"Right." Mackenzie sat where he was, and I walked back across the cricket pitch. I cut through the Botanical Garden on my way back to town and noticed many hummingbirds darting around the flowering shrubs and trees. They were like iridescent, hovering jewels, and several of them made inquisitive passes at my face. When I was almost to the gates, a cannonball tree released one of its globules and it thudded into the ground. As I turned into the road, I wondered if the things ever fell on anybody's head—they were heavy.

It was only eight o'clock when I turned into the lobby of the Fort Young Hotel, but Roseau was already beginning to heat up like a furnace. The hotel had been built on the original foundations of an old fort, and somebody had demonstrated considerable taste and spent a lot of money. Beyond the lobby was a pool, shaded by a trellis with what appeared to be orchids all over it, and fountains splashing. A freshwater swimming pool was beyond the unsided bar, and to the right, a large dining room with its inner side open and its street side ventilated by the actual embrasures from the old fort.

I had breakfast there, admiring the profusion of anthurium lilies which graced every table, and the other tropic blooms which stood in polished brass measuring tubs of the nineteenth century. The service was deft, the food good, and I realized that someone had done a training job. I had paid my bill and was ready to go when I heard a loud shriek, feminine, from the poolside beyond the bar.

I walked out and saw a tall blonde in a sun-faded orange bikini and skimpy bra hit the water in a flat racing dive, and go storming toward the far end of the pool with an expert crawl stroke and tremendous flutter-kicking propulsion. She was being pursued by three *café-au-lait* fellows who could not begin to match her stroke.

It was too much of a coincidence. *There can't be that many blond, thirtyish amazons in this area,* I thought. Going into the bar, I ordered another coffee and watched the disporting swimmers. When the big girl hit the far end of the pool, she went over its edge like an otter and stood there laughing, tucking down her tiny bikini edges, which threatened to come right off her shapely ass, and tucking up the insufficient halter.

Motioning to the black waiter, I asked him who the attractive swimmer was. He told me she was Martha Stock, a white lady who lived in St. Sauteurs, but often visited Dominica. I thanked him, and asked if he would tell her that a fellow American would like to buy her a drink or coffee. He nodded and walked toward the other end of the pool.

When she came to the table in the corner of the bar, still laughing and toweling at her hair, I got up. Asked her what she would like, and when she said a lime squash, ordered it. I introduced myself by my cover name and told her how much I was enjoying Dominica.

"Isn't it divine?" she asked. "They'll ruin it, of course, when Holiday Inn and Hilton get the word, but now it is quite the best spot in the Caribbean. And I'm not a Yank, actually, but a Canadian."

I nodded as the waiter put her iced drink down. When he was out of earshot I said, "I know. And if you're not back on board *Romany* almost immediately, I'm going to walk down the street to the cable office and pull your current charter right out from under you."

"My God!" Her hands flew up. "Just my rotten luck. You're the man."

"That's not the point," I said patiently. "You were directed not to come ashore here. You're being paid your full charter price for at least a month, or as long as I need you. But only to follow orders. Mackenzie tells me you're a good skipper, but I don't like women captains. They do stupid things like you are doing now."

The blue eyes narrowed in her tanned face as she lifted the lime squash, sipped it, and inspected me. "My, you're a nasty article, aren't you? Did some unfeeling lady stomp on your gonads or something, once upon a time?"

"A legion of them," I said. "All wearing golf shoes with cleats."

"That must leave you very short on performance," she said.

"Not really. I fake it pretty good."

Martha Stock leaned back and laughed. I don't mean she giggled or had a burst of suppressed mirth. I mean her long tanned legs flew apart, and she laughed from the umbilicus. You can't keep being stern with a lady like that.

"Will you please," I asked, "get back on board and follow the orders that were a condition of the charter."

"That I will," she said, and as I got up, flashed me an openhanded British salute.

"Thanks." I walked out of the Fort Young Hotel, and stood staring across the street at the white splendor of Government House and its huge garden. Going down the street past the Liat office and Mackenzie's Safari headquarters, I saw two of his Land Rovers pull out, loaded with tourists. The native drivers wore African hunter's hats with flaring brims.

I was going past the open-air market with its rusting

columns and roof when another of the Safari drivers caught up with me.

"Sah," he said. "Please to go back to Mackenzie's, in the rear."

I nodded and turned. The back entrance led through a narrow alley choked with garbage, and wound up in a small courtyard which seemed to be a laundry. I was sitting on one of the concrete tubs when Ian came out the back door.

"This place stinks," I said, and he lifted his patrician nose and sampled the air.

"Isn't that odd? Guess I've been here too long. Smells quite normal to me."

"You've been here too long," I assured him. One of the water taps was half-turned on, and I closed it.

"This just came," he said, handing me a folded piece of notepaper. "One of the little black wharf rats, the boys who dive for coins off the wharf, brought it."

The wharf rat's hands had been wet; the note was damp and nearly illegible. It seemed hastily scrawled and was unsigned. "Jn Ratoon and the blck dwarf are going to the Emerald Pool." I read it over twice and looked up at Mackenzie. The note had to be from Clarrie Ramjohn.

"Where's the Emerald Pool?"

"About twelve miles up, on the road. Another two miles off the road. Slippery going, though."

"Have you got a car that can take me up there?"

"Certainly."

"Do you have any small arms?"

Ian hesitated. "A Colt .38 Police Special, smuggled in. You could get me in trouble with this government."

"I want it. I'll buy you out of the government trouble, if there is any."

He nodded, went back into his office, and came back with an oiled holster holding the pistol. I took it out, checked the load and action. It was in good shape, and had been well-cared for. Best of all, he had not mentioned any price. In my mind, it was automatically doubled. I told him about meeting and admonishing Martha Stock in the hotel, and he laughed involuntarily.

"Man," I said, "let's have less local color and more performance."

"Right." His levity faded, and he said he would have a Land Rover pick me up at the alley entrance. I shoved the holstered pistol into my waistband, nodded, and started walking toward it.

The driver, resplendent in his flaring hat with the leopard skin ribbon, bush jacket, and khaki shorts, was named Augustus. As the Land Rover went humming upward and around the sharp switch-back corners, I looked out over long tropic valley vistas, which were as beautiful as anything Tahiti had to offer. We passed the roundabout, where the main road led off to the airport, and took a smaller one.

Several miles later Augustus stopped the Land Rover and we got out and began walking into a dense tropic forest. For the first half mile, planks and split sections of logs had been laid down along the marshy path. After that, we wound around immense gommier trees which blotted out the sky, crossed three suspension bridges with slippery foot-treads, and finally started down a path so steep you had to cling to ferns to keep from falling.

A faint roaring of falling water began to be heard, and after another half hour of careful foot placement, we emerged in a green glade. Down below was a lagoon of clear water, fed by a pluming waterfall from the rock ledges above. We went down toward the lagoon laboriously, over slippery rocks.

Above us, above the waterfall which created the emerald pool, was a valley planted in young sugarcane.

Its stalks rippled in pale green, from the trade winds
we did not get below at the pool. I sat down on one
of the damp boulders fringing the hidden lagoon, because the trip through the dense forest was a test for
trained athletes. And I was an old lag, breathing
heavily, paying the toll of too much drink and cigarettes.

Nothing moved where we were. No breeze, although
the cane above was still rippling. I glanced at Augustus
and saw he was not watching me. He was looking up
at the waterfall. I followed his gaze and saw two
figures standing on the lowest ledge above the falls.

One of them was the black dwarf. The other was
dressed like a Dominican field hand, and he held a
cutlass in his left hand and a carbine in his right. Looking at him, I had a queer sense of recognition. I knew
he must be John Ratoon, but he was somebody else,
too. Somebody I knew. They were both watching me,
the dwarf with his wide mouth slack.

"We meet again, Captain Jack," said the tall Negro
dressed as a laborer. When he said it, I remembered
the timbre of his voice very well. On my last contract
assignment, in the States, he had been named Ahmed 4
and had done his best to kill me after I had infiltrated
his guerrilla movement. "What are you, my personal
nemesis dispatched from whitey's headquarters every
time I move?"

"No," I said. "It was just another assignment. I had
no idea you were John Ratoon."

He started down the trail beside the waterfall, slashing at vines with his cutlass. "You fucked me up good
in the States, Captain Jack. Got my best people killed,
and my whole movement crippled."

The black dwarf was lurching along behind him, half-
sliding down the narrow trail. Ahmed said he knew
where the pistol was, and where I had gotten it. Not
to try, even.

He crouched at the edge of the lagoon and snapped his fingers. The dwarf lighted him a cigarette and passed it over. Ahmed threw it into the pool, shouted something in patois I could not follow, and the humbled dwarf lighted him a thick cigar. The lean black man drew hard on it, squatting and gazing at me.

"Why did you follow me?" he insisted. I repeated I hadn't; that I was on assignment and had no idea that John Ratoon was Ahmed 4. He puffed on the big cigar again, considering this.

"What can you gain?" I asked. "Publicity, yes. What else?"

"You don't understand the West Indian mind, Captain Jack," he said. "The history of these islands is the fire right now. For centuries rebellious slaves burned cane fields. They burned whole towns, often just to create work in rebuilding them. So we don't intend to change the pattern. When we grab all these cruise ships, planes, yachts, whatever offers, we're going to burn them."

I thought how many millions of dollars would be lost if that was done. "And all the thousands of stranded passengers, what about them?"

"What about them?" asked the crouching revolutionary. "We black people have always been told they were Christlike. Let them walk upon the water."

I didn't comment.

"I'm tired of your interference," Ahmed said. "You won't leave this island alive." Shrugged. "On the other hand, you won't be killed until the *Federal Palm* is far from here. Okay, boss man?"

I stood watching him. He was in a patch of sunlight, and a hummingbird darted at his face. He brushed the hovering sprite away. It was a garnet-throated type with a brilliant gorget, crimson feathers with gold reflections, a black bill and feet. Its wing coverts were rich green with bronze shadings.

"Like this," he said, and puffed on his thick cigar until its tip glowed. The hummingbird made another pass at his face, and he deliberately offered it the cigar tip. The darting bird, like flashing fire, came back and its forked tongue jammed into the glowing tip. With a strangled chirp the hummingbird plunged into an erratic orbit, ever diminishing, and smashed to the ground. There it lay dying, in a tousled spread of feathers, all atremble.

"You're next, Captain Jack," said Ahmed. When he whistled, men with cutlasses started coming out of the cane field.

Acting on orders from

Ratoon-Ahmed, the black troopers dressed like Dominican field hands slashed down lianas, and he personally tied my hands behind my back with the slippery vines. At the point of his carbine, I was forced back down the sunless, damp trail. I slipped and fell twice on the waterlogged boardwalk, and both times Ratoon triggered his carbine carelessly by my head, into the forest mould. Augustus, the Safari driver, was being herded along behind me, and he also went down several times but did not get the scorching blast of gunfire.

When we were back at the road, I was panting again and dripping with sweat. A truck was waiting, and Ratoon got rope from it and trussed my feet as well. When that was done, four of the troopers heaved me up on the truck bed. I heard a shout and saw that Augustus had made a break toward the jungle. Ratoon wheeled and chopped down on him with the carbine.

The guide was hit and half-spun; he blundered to his knees, lunged up again at another angle, and as carbine slugs kept slashing the tall grass around him, went diving into the lush foliage.

Ratoon cursed. He had emptied a clip but swiftly replaced it, tossed the weapon to one of the troopers, and ordered two others to accompany him in pursuit. They went charging through the grass and were lost to sight under the shadowing gommier trees. Ratoon said something in the singsong French-African-English patois I could not follow, and swung behind the wheel of the truck. As it started, the other ragged troopers swarmed aboard.

We went higher up in the mountains, toward the cloud-wreathed summit of Diablotin, and the road became walled by pluming fern forests and mountain palms. The air became noticeably cooler, and the sun was blotted out by low-hanging clouds. I was trying to calculate the mileage and direction; after another couple of miles Ratoon turned off the main road into a dirt side-lane so overgrown I would not have noticed it. The rank growth, high as the truck's cab, clattered past and closed behind us.

Another two miles down the remote side-track and the truck stopped. At an order from Ratoon, I was rolled off the truck bed and arched my back to keep from hitting the ground headfirst. Cutlasses chopped down a ten-foot section of bamboo, and this was laid across my fetters and lashed tight by more hacked-down fronds. Trussed like a shot tiger, I was carried up a grassy knoll.

There the bamboo pole was unshouldered and I was dumped to the ground again. While another parley in the patois began, I twisted over on one shoulder and saw that we were just below the mushrooming base of an abandoned and topless stone sugar mill. The narrowed top was a serrated rampart, open to the sky, but a massive tree beyond the mill arched its waxen green branches above it.

"Goddammit!" shouted Ratoon angrily, in English, "I don't want him dead before I get off this island . . ."

The patois jabber began again. He strode angrily to the truck, got a rope, and jerking the bamboo pole loose, lashed it around my wrists. I was carried to the top of the knoll, and the rope passed over a low branch of the tree. Then, while Ratoon shouted orders, I was hoisted and dropped down into the ruined sugar mill. Or almost down. When I was about eight feet from its floor, dangling and turning, the rope was slashed by a trooper and I plummeted the rest of the way.

I landed with my knees bent and fell face forward, because I could not fling my bound hands forward in time. The earth at the bottom of the old mill was damp and stank of rotting bagasse, the crushed remnants of cane, mixed with red volcanic soil. I slipped over on my back and stared up at the ragged stone rampart.

A frieze of dark faces was staring down at me. Ratoon, flanked by his troopers; I realized that they must have driven the truck up the slope and were standing on its bed. I had not heard the truck start, but on the other hand I had hit the floor with considerable force. The faces were unsmiling.

"This tree above your little hidey-hole," called Ratoon conversationally, "is called the manchineel. It is feared all through these islands because its resin is a poisonous caustic." He was speaking with the same precision he had used on the hidden grenade range in Georgia. "If you walk under it when rain is falling, your skin will blister. If you break a branch and get the juice in your eye, Braille City, Captain Jack. So you better pray for a drought . . ."

I surveyed the arching green branches. Drought was

unlikely in the high interior of Dominica; the annual rainfall there was over three hundred inches, challenging upper Burma as the wettest spot in the world.

"Wouldn't want to go off and leave you lonely," added Ratoon-Ahmed from the rampart. What looked like an animated cluster of dark green sugarcanes was emptied from a crate above. The writhing cluster struck the damp floor of the mill and separated into four angry and striking green snakes, each about eight feet long.

After they had rolled over, each snake thrust up the wedge-shaped head of the pit viper, and my guts congealed with terror. The high-held heads were swinging, hanging like javelins, and long fangs protruded from beneath their scaly jaws and licking black tongues.

"I wouldn't use them for pillows," suggested Ratoon from above. "These fellows are mean. Call them fer-de-lance. With the green mamba, they're one of the few which will attack man without provocation. So in case of a knockdown, Captain Jack, go to the nearest neutral corner. Two drops of their venom, baby, causes painful death. *Oh, shit!* I forgot you ain't got no corners down there . . ."

His head withdrew and I heard him shouting orders. Then it reappeared.

"Have to go now, Cap'n," he said, as blandly as if he had just met an old friend in a bar. "Nice seeing you again, but I have to get back aboard ship, before she sails. Incidentally, the reason you had no luck latchin' on to me aboard the *Palm* was because I was wood-sheddin' in the cabin next to yours. Happened to be vacant . . . You were pretty cute about the hash switch but were never a real threat. Our people made you the minute you landed in Montego Bay . . .

"You get so intense with your orders from the Head Whitey, Captain Jack, that you forget you've poisoned a lot of stews. You're a celebrity, man, face it. A prick, but a celebrated prick. Now, because that Safari cat bolted, and maybe wasn't hit well enough to die in the jungle, I got to get sudden on . . .

"Be dark down there soon, but don't count on that for protection. Old fer-de-lance is nocturnal, hunts at night. Like I'm going to hunt tonight, to see that Clarrie Ramjohn slut goes overboard between here and St. Lucia."

He paused. "If you ain't dead by morning, my men will come back and shoot you. Won't be hard from up here."

His head vanished, the truck started, and I heard it go thrashing back through the growth. The sky was darkening above the manchineel tree. As I waited, lying trussed and on my back, rain began to spatter on its glossy green leaves. I edged back toward the flaring stone wall of the mill. Unless we had a drenching downpour, I might be able to avoid the water dripping from its branches.

As I began to saw both wrists, not suddenly, against the constricting lianas, I was watching the fer-de-lances. I didn't want to startle them, because if I did and got bitten, I would die very soon. They had colonized across the damp earth floor, but were still reared up and ready to strike.

One of my studies had been herpetology, and as I worked my arms slowly and patiently, I tried to remember what I had read about the fer-de-lance . . . They are the color of green velvet, with darker V's along the slender body. A ridge from the pointed snout to behind the eyes, which are also greenish with jet-black, elliptical pupils . . .

Watching the four weaving, wedge-shaped heads, I remembered that they could strike farther than any other snake. Their enormous fangs are half as long as the head, are retractable, and when striking, are pointed forward. The fer-de-lance has for centuries been responsible for most of the snakebite deaths in the Caribbean Islands, Central America, and northern South America. The female bears up to seventy-five young, all of whom are fully armored with lethal poison at birth.

I cannot tell how long it took, probably twenty minutes, to free my wrists. Then carefully, slowly, I checked my pockets in the fading light. Fortunately, Ratoon had not really searched me; he had just patted me down for a weapon, after taking the pistol. I still had my butane cigarette lighter, and some incidental papers and currency. Also, a packet of folder matches I had picked up while having breakfast in the Fort Young Hotel. They were not paper matches, but sulfur-tipped slivers of wood, made in Belgium.

I was looking at them when one of the fer-de-lance came slithering across the damp floor at me. I struck a match and flipped it at him. He stopped and reared angrily. I scratched another and flipped it at him, but it went out. Still, the lesson was there. Fire was my only protection.

I surveyed the contents of my emptied pockets. I had my passport, olive green and oily to the touch. My yellow, stiff folder of International Certificates of Vaccination, some U.S. bank notes and forty-odd dollars in East Caribbean Authority "Biwee" dollars. Money to burn. Or at least I hoped the friggin' stuff would burn . . . Nothing more inflammable, and for the first time I cursed the absence of junk mail, which plagues most householders.

The international health certificate was made of strong cardboard paper, so I carefully tore it into small pieces. It had eight small pages, and I blessed the bureaucrat who had dreamed it up. By now it was almost fully dark in the bottom of the abandoned sugar mill, and when I lighted the small pile of stiff, yellow paper fragments, I felt like an aging boy scout seeking a merit badge for survival.

The torn pile of yellow scraps flared, burned brightly for a moment, and then died. I flipped the lighter again, and this time it stayed lighted. The fer-de-lance which had come across to attack me, and which was now only three feet away, kept his distance. But the poison fangs were still levered forward, and the head was still swinging . . .

Full darkness came. I methodically tore the pages out of my passport and built small fires of them. When the covers would not burn, I cursed them and began shredding the bank notes. The wind began to rage outside, and a torrential rain began hammering through the branches of the manchineel tree. Because the opening at the top of the sugar mill was much smaller than its ballooned bottom, I did not at first feel the effects of it. Then, as the moisture dripping from the branches began to pervade the dirt floor, I felt my buttocks and supporting hands begin to sting.

I knew that every drop would raise a blister, and hunched back as far as I could against the arching wall. I had nowhere else to go. There was some runoff through the porous volcanic soil, but it was not enough to help. And it made my building of small protective fires much more difficult . . .

Finally, with my skin stinging all over, I was building them doggedly in one shoe, and then another. That didn't help much. They burned well enough, for a while, inside the shoes, but these containers were too sodden to keep them alight. Over my tiny flames, I could still see the fer-de-lance. The one nearest me had not retreated; his ugly head swung like a pendulum every time I struck a match or flipped the wheel of my lighter.

I do not know how many of these small protective beacons I lighted. I did it methodically, hoping that the butane lighter I had filled the night before on the *Federal Palm* would hold out. I did it delicately, like a watchmaker examining a mainspring. Because I had the surety that if the lighter missed fire or I fell asleep, I would be dead before dawn.

My lighter quit work-

ing about two hours later. When it did, I sat quietly
in the darkness, listening for the rustle of the fer-de-
lance. I was no longer frightened of them, because fear
cannot be sustained that long. I was hoping that I
would be able to strangle a couple of the spade-headed
bastards before the venom took effect, when a voice
echoed down to me. A flashlight beam probed around
from the jagged rampart overhead, and stopped on me.

"Turn that goddamned light off," I said, not shouting
but in a raised voice. The light was snapped off.

"Ian Mackenzie here," announced the invisible figure
above.

"God bless Ian Mackenzie," I answered steadily.
Added that I needed matches and something flammable,
a weapon. Did he have any?

"Matches and paper, yes. No firearms. The only

77

one I had was the pistol I gave you. Have a cutlass in the truck."

"Then that's it. Lash them all to the hook on that front bumper winch. Drop the hook a few feet down into the mill, being sure the line is seated so it won't foul on a crack in the stonework. Don't use the power on the winch; I don't want that much noise. Lower it by hand, and wait for the word on the flashlight."

"Right." I got to my feet cautiously, and kept pawing toward the darkness at the center of the mill. For what seemed an eternity. I could feel nothing, and when I sneezed involuntarily I heard the snakes moving.

"Where is the fucking thing, Ian?" I called.

"I've got about thirty feet rolled off the drum. It ought to be within reach."

"I can't find it. Snap your torch on it, then off."

The flashlight's beam stabbed downward, and off. In its brief illumination I had seen the hook, with the cutlass dangling from it. And the other things bundled in a handkerchief, swinging slowly, just beyond my outstretched hands. And the fer-de-lance, too, almost under it, their heads high and also swinging.

I could not grab the hook without stepping within their striking range.

"Stone the crows!" said Ian from above. "Have you been down there all night with those slimy bastards?"

"Mackenzie," I said, "we'll chat another time. I've had a very colorful life, but it might end right here. I can't reach the hook; they're too close to it and too excited. Have you got some petrol you can reach easily?"

"Yes. A can of it strapped to the Rover."

"If I retreat to the wall," I asked, "can you ignite a piece of cloth soaked in petrol and drop it between me and these aroused serpents?"

"I think so, yes. If they don't move, of course."

"Do it. And old friend, bowl me a googly, please."

"Righto." I heard him move away from the rampart, and slowly went back myself until I was pressed against the cold stones. Several minutes later a flaming bundle fell to the center of the mill's floor, striking the nearest fer-de-lance on the head. I had a bad moment when I thought he might be blinded and come lashing toward me, but he and the other snakes rippled the other way, hissing.

I took four steps, snatched the steel hook, and unloaded it. After building another small fire, crouching and staring at the angry snakes, I made a loop of the winch cable, passed it under my butt, and tied the hook secure with the same small rope Ian had sent down. Up above, he was monitoring my actions by the flickering light of the small fire and keeping a steady handstrain on the cable. I blessed the Scotsman as a good and knowledgeable man.

"Now the power on the winch," I called, and heard him retreating to the truck, still keeping the line taut. The Land Rover started, the cable tightened, and I was hoisted upward, holding the cutlass ready and watching the fer-de-lance. The fire was dying down, but still keeping them at bay. Its ruddy light flickered in their dark eyes.

As we went bouncing back down the overgrown pathway, with shrubs and tall grass slapping at the Rover's sides, Mackenzie explained that when neither myself nor his driver returned, he had gone looking. Had found Augustus, the driver, sprawled unconscious in the road halfway up Mount Diablotin. He had two wounds in the lower back, and was presently in the Roseau Hospital; after a transfusion, he had been able to talk, haltingly, before going out again.

"A good man," I said bitterly. "He broke toward the jungle, and that bastard of a Ratoon shot him in the back." I added that if Augustus needed to be flown out to Jamaica, or Trinidad, or even the States, the agency would pay for the flight and any medical attention required.

"Right," said Ian. He added that from what he had learned in Augustus's brief period of lucidity, he had checked every side road further up Mount Diablotin. After nearly giving up, he had found one which had flattened growth, where Ratoon's truck had driven in and out.

"Pretty fair tracking," I commented. "Considering it was night, overcast, and you hadn't much of a clue. My thanks. I couldn't have lasted until morning."

Mackenzie nodded. Without warning, my hands began to tremble; without volition, they flew up out of my lap. I began shaking like a dog coming out of water. I suppose it was because I had been under tight control too long but, for whatever reason, I couldn't stop shaking. Mackenzie reached over me into the panel stowage compartment and handed me a bottle of rum.

I got the top off all right, but then had trouble hitting my mouth with the neck of the bottle. Finally I took a scalding blast, thought my gut would rebel, but weathered that storm and the panic dissolved in warmth. Baring my teeth, I waited a few minutes and had another belt; that helped even more.

A light rain was falling as we drove past the Rose's lime juice factory, across the iron bridge, and stopped before the darkened Safari offices. We went inside, but Mackenzie did not turn on any lights. He did go to the far wall and flip the switches of his ship-to-shore radio equipment, and the dials glowed dimly. On voice, he called *Romany Two,* the racing yacht skippered by Martha Stock.

She answered immediately, and I wondered what she was doing up at that hour. It was almost 4:00 a.m. Ian requested an immediate rendezvous off Scot's Head, on the south end of Dominica. A boat to be put ashore on the Caribbean side.

"Will do," agreed Martha Stock. Her voice sounded efficient coming through the receiver, falling into the darkened office. "Take us . . . a little more than an hour to get there. Give the dinghy twenty minutes to get ashore."

"Right. Thank you and out." Ian Mackenzie flipped the switches again, the dials went dark. "So what else?" he asked me.

"The next request is personal. My feet, scalp, and shoulders are stinging like a bitch from the rain filtered through that manchineel tree over the mill. Have you got someplace I could wash, and some clothes I could use?"

The Scotsman looked me over, as well as he could in the dimness. Faint illumination from the lights outside the Fort Young Hotel fell through the shuttered windows. We were about the same size and height.

"I have some khakis here. We could go to my house, but I have two servants living in. They'd know."

"The khakis will be fine," I said, "and I can sluice off in those laundry tubs in the back."

He nodded, and from a bottom drawer in his desk drew out a bush jacket and some khaki shorts. He had no bath soap, but after we had searched the cleaning woman's closet we found half a box of Breeze detergent. Clutching it, I said that was a hell of a way to run a safari, and he answered that not many of his clients spent the night under the dread manchineel tree. They were protected from such dangers . . .

There was some truth in what he said. I retired to the back courtyard, and, crouching in one of the concrete washbasins, sluiced water over my stinging body until I had worked up a Breeze lather. When it was

washed off, I felt enormously better, and used my old
garments to dry between the toes, as I had been instructed to do since childhood. Then I remembered
that I was just transferring the caustic, so I soaped and
washed again. This time, Ian brought me a towel from
his Land Rover.

When I was snugging up the shorts and shrugging
into the bush jacket, he brought me back a new pair
of thonged rubber sandals.

"Bata?" I asked, fitting my toes into them.

"Right."

"How much here?"

"About a $1.40, Biwee."

I considered the price. It was more than twice what
the thonged sandals, made by the same company, cost
in the United States. There, in the discount houses,
they cost thirty-three cents a pair. So much for the
undeveloped areas.

"Let's go," I said.

We passed through the darkened office, got back in
the Land Rover, and rolled out toward Scot's Head.
As we left Roseau, twisting through mean and narrow
streets, I asked Mackenzie to cable the Castries police
in St. Lucia as soon as the cable office was open. Ask-
ing them to issue a warrant for the arrest of John Ratoon, assistant purser of the *Federal Palm,* when it arrived. For manslaughter, immediately, and a possible
following charge of murder in the first degree, if
Augustus died.

Ian nodded. We passed through two small villages
with every door and window tightly closed, and fishing
boats drawn up on the narrow beaches above the tide
mark. Came, finally, to the narrow and rocky promon-
tory of Scot's Head, where the surf smashes in from the
Atlantic side and murmurs in from the Caribbean.

Mackenzie cut the ignition, and we were left with the trade winds rustling around the Land Rover.

"There'll be a bonus for helping me," I said. "A big one. But that has fuck-all to do with anything. I'm grateful."

"Oh . . ." He offered me a cigarette, took one himself, and lighted them. It was beginning to be dawn. "Matter of happenstance, mostly, isn't it? I mean, people get in trouble, so there you are . . ." His thin face was drawn; I knew he had been up a long time.

"No," I said. "Not that cozy. You went out of your way . . ."

He nodded, staring at the brightening sea.

Even in the dawning light, we never saw *Romany Two's* black hull. But in an hour her dinghy, lashed by a big Merc outboard, came to the Caribbean beach. There were two black seamen in it. I shook hands with Ian Mackenzie, thanked him again, and the dinghy took me aboard and went winging back toward *Romany Two,* offshore and not visible from Dominica.

Martha Stock had

changed her image. The tall Canadian girl had looked like a sorry by-product of a cut-rate jet set beside the pool in Dominica, but now her blond hair was drawn back in a severe bun. She wore a short-sleeved blouse and tattered shorts. And when she gave orders to the black seamen, it was with easy, profane authority. They were used to it, and jumped to the numbers.

I told her that our destination was St. Lucia, and she nodded and said we had a favoring wind. While I watched, she and the crew rigged ship and hoisted the anchor. *Romany* heeled over as her sails filled, and went spanking away with the breeze. When she had set the course and instructed the helmsman, Miss Stock came down to the luxurious cabin salon, where I was sitting at the teakwood bar and sipping at her black Jack Daniel's.

"Some canoe you've got here," I said.

"Isn't she nice?" She was smiling, and it transformed her tanned face. No makeup at all, and you could see the good bone structure. *A racehorse,* I thought, *built for the route . . .*

"Three big double staterooms," she added proudly. "Captain's quarters and cabin space for five crewmen, although we only use three on short charters. Carl and I had three smaller craft and another *Romany* before we could build up to this one. She's got all our ideas in her, and most of them work."

"Carl's your brother, he of the broken leg?"

"Right. The drunken lout . . ." She said it in such an affectionate way that I wished, briefly, that I had someone, somewhere, to malign me so. "And yes, Mr. Miles, to complete your dossier, I have been married twice . . ."

"Oh?"

"Yes. Nice lads, too, but lightly ballasted. They ran out of gas." She went behind the bar and mixed herself a Scotch and soda, humming.

Watching her deft movements, the clean lines of her body under the sketchy singlet and ragged shorts, I wondered just how tough her men had to be. It was an interesting conjecture. As if she could read my mind, the tall girl smiled, not looking at me, and spoke again.

"Nothing goes with the charter, Mr. Miles, except the yacht and its services."

"Bless my soul, Miss Martha," I answered, returning her smile. "I would never try to trade on our propinquity. And besides, you're probably stronger than I am."

"I doubt it. But at least your thoughts are commendably wholesome."

That having been established, I took another tack. "Why five coffee-grinder winches?"

"Oh, they're the difference, you see, in a close race. Quite helpful."

"I see. I'm sure you're aware, Miss Stock, that the charter made for me is corporate, although I may be the only person using *Romany*. My work, my use of the yacht, stem from objectives which are urgent and private."

The scrubbed blonde with the good bones nodded. "I'm aware of that. All you have to do is tell me what you want. So long as it will not endanger *Romany* or contravene law, I will do it."

"Good," I said heartily. "First, how will you explain taking me off Dominica without any customs or immigration clearance?"

The shapely sea captain stared at me and then broke up, laughing ruefully.

"No matter," I assured her. "I was only an in-transit passenger on the *Federal Palm*. They didn't have me listed as being on the island."

"You," she announced crisply, freshening her drink, "are a confusing bastard . . . Trapping me like that."

I was liking her more and more; her reactions were masculine, and I couldn't help wondering if the failed marriages meant she had a touch of butch. I hoped not, because it would have meant a great waste . . .

When I asked if she could use the key, she nodded and said she held all the licenses. Then I asked if she could work Washington, D. C., direct, and she nodded again. Said she could work Iceland direct, if I needed it. I told her that I was going to encode a long message, to be sent CW to Washington, and that it would have to go off as soon as I had it written.

She nodded again, and led me down to a luxurious double stateroom. Switched on the lights, including one over a polished rosewood desk. Asked if I wanted the ports closed and the air conditioning turned on. *Ro-*

many was skipping to the favoring wind so smoothly that a stream of cool air poured through the stateroom, so I said no. She went out, and I had a shower because my skin was still tingling from the moisture I had absorbed, indirectly, from the manchineel tree.

Sitting naked at the rosewood desk, I did two drafts of my urgent report to Neal Pearsall, head of the agency's action division. I said in it that I had collided with John Ratoon of the *Federal Palm,* whom Neal would remember as Ahmed 4 in the black guerrilla contract, the training-cadre leader of The Republic of New Africa Movement in the States.

That because he had thought me safely stowed away and soon to be a victim of ritual murder, Ratoon-Ahmed had boasted that his new revolutionary movement in the Caribbean Islands would soon seize, simultaneously, all communications in the lesser islands of Antigua, Montserrat, Dominica, St. Lucia, St. Vincent, and St. Sauteurs. In addition his locally recruited Black Power radicals would take over, on the day, all aircraft, cruise ships, freighters, and incidental shipping, such as yachts, and interisland sloops and schooners.

That Ratoon-Ahmed had flatly stated that the purpose of his movement was not to just generate worldwide headlines, but that all the facilities and transport would be burned. Passengers would be stranded, and his troops had no intention of helping them in any way. He had further implied that his men could take over the governments of most of the small Caribbean islands, and meant to do so.

My suggestions were: that the Department of Defense immediately assemble seven platoons of black paratroopers, with black officers. At the same time, the State Department should advise the governments of the smaller Windward Islands of a possible coup and a simultaneous attempt to take over their transport and communications facilities. That these governments be invited to accept an official visit of the black platoons, which would in no island amount to more than 130 troopers, and in the smaller ones, like Montserrat, to not more than 65.

These black cadres could pass in review before the various Prime Ministers and/or Governors or Governors-General of the small islands, and their officers would present goodwill plaques to the dignitaries.

I stressed that such a show of the U.S. flag in the larger islands was obviously impermissible, as had been shown by our recent bad world press when elements of the fleet stood off Trinidad's shores when its regiment mutinied. But the poorhouse islands, lush in greenery as they were, would be both relieved and appreciative to have this token presence at hand on the date of the proposed coup.

I reminded Pearsall that the Caribbean Federation had been scuttled several years ago by Jamaica, Trinidad, and Barbados, because they did not want their bankrupt little black brothers slung around their necks like an economic albatross.

I advised the following disposition of the black paratroop platoons, by Globemaster, as soon as possible: Montserrat, after consultation with the British Foreign Office, one platoon; Dominica, one platoon; St. Lucia, two platoons, or 130 men; St. Vincent, one platoon; and St. Sauteurs, two platoons.

I made no recommendation about Antigua, because its unrest was so severe and its population so surly that I did not think we could affect an attempted coup without massive intervention.

Finally, I suggested that the same Globemasters that delivered the platoons should remain on standby alert until the order came for them to remove the troopers as swiftly as they had arrived. Nothing else was needed, and in my opinion, no international incident would be created. Principally because nobody gave much of a damn about these bankrupt islands; ten determined men with baseball bats could probably take them over, if nobody was watching. But a swift shuttle of trained Negro soldiers, even in small cadres, would stop Ratoon's revolutionaries cold.

Further, all shipping companies and airlines that would have vessels or aircraft in the Caribbean area during the next thirty days should install passengers who were actually armed guards, at whatever expense and in sufficient numbers, to repel boarders attempting to take over. I cautioned against extending this same warning to yacht marinas and private craft, on the grounds that it would inevitably spread the news prematurely.

I acknowledged that I did not know the exact target date for Ratoon's Caribbean take-over, but suspected it was imminent. And that my confrontation with him, and my escape from his murder scheme, might even accelerate the date.

I reported that I could not tell whether he had sufficient backing to attempt his bold bid in the larger islands of Jamaica, Barbados, and Trinidad. He had sizeable numbers of followers in these larger islands, but they also had relatively stable economies, if now depressed, trained troops, and a constabulary of sorts. In Trinidad, especially, the Black Power movement had already torn the island apart with looting, arson, and a mutiny in the only regiment.

It was my belief that all diplomatic and banking representatives, plus the white officers of international companies, should be warned immediately to hire armed guards for themselves and their families. Only a week ago, as agency reports from there would indicate, the normally tranquil island of Tobago, off Trinidad, had erupted with a savage Black Power riot. Militants from Trinidad had invaded hotels, spat on and abused white tourists, torn up a golf course, and done senseless damage to a multi-million-dollar hotel under construction.

As a result, the international chain that had been financing the hotel had announced that it would not complete it. They were withdrawing entirely. All hotels and guest houses on Tobago were empty, and white residents who had lived on that lovely little island for generations were preparing to leave. Three days ago, the Trinidad Hilton, 231 rooms, had had exactly 95 guests, considerably less than the staff employed by that luxury inn.

That I was proceeding on the chartered yacht *Romany Two* from Dominica to Castries, St. Lucia, and would report from there. That on no account should the actions I suggested be delayed if I did not report in soon. The situation was too dangerous for delay. Please to expedite as written.

Finally, I said, I was aware that my suggestions were on the level of high policy making, and were being forwarded by an agent in the field. That I had considered this, and if State and Defense wished to equivocate as usual, I offered them the dismal prospect of thousands and thousands of U.S., British, and Canadian tourists stranded on hot islands without benefit of mail service, cable office service, or any way to contact their homes or diplomatic representatives.

I did a third draft of the explosive report, and then spent another hour encoding it. When that was done, I tore up the previous drafts and sent their fragments fluttering out the porthole in the bathroom. It was the farthest aft, and I doubted if the bits of paper would be seen from the deck.

When I walked back down the companionway to the

radio shack opening off the main salon, Martha Stock was waiting. The banked wall of communication equipment held glowing, lighted dials. I handed her the four-page message, and she looked it over, after fitting on heavy harlequin-type reading glasses.   She nodded, cleared the key with a practiced fist, and began rattling off a call to the big agency station in Foggy Bottom, Washington.

They answered immediately, as they should have with half a million watts of power, and she nodded again and began sending swiftly.

I got a bottle of black Jack Daniel's, a bucket of ice, two bottles of soda, two limes, and retreated to my palatial stateroom. After I got back in it and had two drinks, I discovered that there was a small refrigerator built into the back of the bar. Admiring this fact, I had several drinks. *Romany* kept bowling along, and, for one of the rare times, I could not invent an enemy anywhere. Nobody was there but me and a few flying fishes . . . Skipping over the white-capped waves outside.

After I had taken half the bottle, the warning clock in my head went off. I put it by and had another shower, feeling mellow. *Romany* didn't have plebian bunks; she had two double beds. I fell into one of them, in a hard, dreamless sleep.

I was awakened by a

persistent knocking on the stateroom door. As I lunged out of bed and went to unlock the door, I noticed bright sunlight at the portholes. The yacht was not moving. Martha Stock was in the companionway, and said she hated to disturb me but that we were hove to, twelve miles off Castries, capital of St. Lucia. She needed some orders. Was *Romany* to enter the harbor?

"No ma'am. But I would like us close enough to send two of your crewmen ashore in the dinghy. Then I'd like them to go into Castries. Can we manage that without being seen?"

The tall blond girl shrugged. "Matter of luck. There's a little bay several miles south of town. They can beach the dinghy there and catch a bus."

"Right. Let's do it."

She nodded. "I thought you secret types were up with the sun. You've slept nearly fourteen hours."

"Only because I knew you were in charge," I said gravely. She smiled at that, and a dimple appeared in her tanned cheeks. "Very attractive, those dimples," I added, and got to see them again.

"Breakfast will be ready whenever you are . . ." She walked away, wearing only a tee shirt and tight shorts, and when I whistled sharply she put a little something extra in it. While I was showering, I heard her swearing at the crewmen like a bosun's mate working lascars. In a few minutes *Romany* heeled into motion again.

After we had put the dinghy over the side with the black seamen in it, the big Merc outboard spun to life and sent it pitching toward the deserted bay. Under auxiliary power *Romany* moved back out beyond the international limit. There, in the blue water of the white-capping Caribbean, Martha and I sat in swivel chairs aft and fished from outrigger lines.

I had just hauled in a thirty-pound dolphin and we were watching its lovely blue-green luster fade to a dismal brown when the remaining black seaman came out of the cabin to report that *Romany* was being called on the voice channel. He had been monitoring the bank of receivers while we fished.

It was Neal Pearsall, calling me from the agency headquarters outside Washington. He said he was on the scrambler phone, and asked if I would have to talk in the clear. I said yes, but wait a minute. I turned and asked Martha if she would take the seaman and go forward, on deck.

"Security?" she asked, and when I nodded she said "not that tough." She flipped the voice receiver off, stabbed a headset jack into the panel, and cleared a mike for me. And then, a smart girl who got the gist of things in one, she took the seaman forward anyway.

"Okay," I said. "Go ahead."

"Where's Ratoon?"

"He left me in Dominica. Worked me over, thought he had arranged my death. Didn't work. We have just put two men ashore, clandestinely, and they will check the news in Castries. But they won't be back until dark. If Ratoon was on the *Palm,* and not hiding, he's under arrest in Castries now. The *Palm* tied up there early this morning. She's scheduled to leave for Barbados at four this afternoon."

"All right. We've checked our files on the Republic of New Africa. From a fast spot-check, a lot of Ratoon-Ahmed's boys are not in the States. Or at least not in their usual addresses. So they may be down there, holed up and waiting for *Der Tag.* Which may be day-after-tomorrow . . .

"A cab driver in St. Vincent decided that he would rather have a new Chevrolet taxi than be a revolutionary hero. He has signed a statement before our man there, Harold Lashley, Minister of Communications, that he is Ratoon's third-in-command on St. Vincent. That his people, forty-three of them, were to take over the airport, radio station, and radar installations at dawn Sunday. The clincher is that he personally led Lashley to an arms cache hidden in a banana plantation. There were enough rapid-fire weapons, grenades, and ammo to outfit fifty men.

"Point Two," continued Pearsall. "We are dispatching now from Mitchell Field sixty-men cadres of black paratroopers. All the smaller islands have agreed to honor their arrival on a state visit, bearing official scrolls of congratulation from the United States on having achieved their freedom and etc. . . . All of them are wearing combat gear, and battle decorations, and their weapons are loaded."

"Good merciful Christ!" I said, honestly astonished. "How did you manage that on such short notice?"

"I am not without low cunning and guile, Joseph," boomed the deep voice smugly. "The Black Power outbreaks in Trinidad, Jamaica, and Tobago have helped, plus the gunning down of the Bosch supporters in Santo Domingo. The cats at State are so nervous they don't even touch their high-piled carpets anymore, just float around over them, whimpering . . .

"Which brings us to Point Three. For the first time since the British left those islands, the big New York banks, First National City and Chase Manhattan, have begun moving in down there. To buck the Barclay's–Canadian–Nova Scotian money monopoly. They are already in Trinidad, Barbados, and Jamaica. First National City plans to open two branches in St. Sauteurs next month. In St. George's, the capital, and Grenville, on the other side of the island.

"On Saturday afternoon, at three o'clock, a U.S. citizen named Fred Sisco has an appointment with the Honorable Eric Ferré, Prime Minister of St. Sauteurs, at Government House. Sisco is thirty-eight, an ex-football star at Cornell, and will be the managing director of St. Sauteur's First National City branches. His wife and his three children will be staying at the Spice Islands Inn, on Grand Anse Beach, while he goes to the official appointment at Government House.

"He won't get there, if our information is correct. A group of Black Power thugs, some of them belonging to the Prime Minister's own 'Mongoose Gang,' a cutrate edition of Haiti's Tontons Macoute, will kidnap him en route. This must not happen. I want you to bypass St. Lucia, St. Vincent, and Barbados, and take off for St. Sauteurs. How soon can you leave for there? What's your time element?"

"*Momentito*," I said. And visualized the geographic position of St. Lucia to St. Sauteurs. It was Thursday; the appointment was Saturday. "I can be in the marina

there late tomorrow night. *Romany's* got twin diesels
in her; if the wind is wrong, but it shouldn't be from
this quarter, she'll do a steady twelve knots. But we
can't leave here until dark tonight, after we pick up the
men who went ashore. This thing can't be worked at
racing pace without them."

"You sound like Captain Bligh," said Pearsall. His
humor is sometimes heavy. "That should give you
plenty of time. Sisco and his family arrive on Liat Airways at 10:20 Saturday morning. How far is it from
the airport to the Spice Islands Inn?"

"About an hour. I can be waiting for him at the hotel."

"That's it, then," said Pearsall.

"Not quite. I can't protect him with coconuts."

"Just a minute." Neal's voice faded as he spoke to
someone in the background. Then he came back on.
"A tailor named Robin on Parish Street, St. George's.
We'll alert him."

"Okay. Are Jamaica, Trinidad, and Barbados in-
cluded in this Sunday dawn grab?"

"We don't know yet, Joseph. But we have alerted
their governments. All of them have sufficient constabulary and police forces to prevent successful seizures.
Trinidad's regiment has been called back to duty, and
seems purged of its recent mutiny. I'm sleeping in my
office, boyo, and staying hooked up to the station.
Please report to me when you clear St. Lucia."

"I'll do that, sir," I replied. "And in conclusion I
just want you to know that I appreciate your attitude
during this whole trying affair. If I were queer, I would
ask your hand in marriage, fake leg and all."

"Balls!" said Pearsall, and hung up.

Late that afternoon

Romany Two went back toward St. Lucia under auxiliary power, throttled down, and it was dusk when we
made the rendezvous with her dinghy. The seamen reported to Martha Stock and she to me, in the salon bar.
The news out of Castries was bad.

John Ratoon had not been arrested. He had not
been found, although a warrant had been issued and
served on the *Federal Palm* before anyone was allowed
ashore. A thorough search of the ship had not turned
him up, and I wondered if he had been sitting inside
the narrow passenger cabin again, next to the one I
had occupied.

Without comment, Martha handed me a flimsy copy
of the *Voice of St. Lucia,* the island paper which had
come out that afternoon. The paper was crudely
printed, as if turned out by careless monkeys working

on a free-form art expression. I went immediately to the small, boxed story on the front page.

STEWARDESS LOST AT SEA

The West Indian Shipping Association's M.V. "Federal Palm" docked here this morning on her biweekly southern-bound visit to Castries and reported the disappearance, en route from Dominica, of Miss Claribelle Ramjohn, 26, a stewardess. Miss Ramjohn, a native of Trinidad, had worked on the ship for four years, since the inception of its Caribbean service with its sister ship, "The Federal Maple." Both vessels were gifts of the Canadian government to the Caribbean Islands. Until further investigations can be made, Miss Ramjohn will be listed as having been lost overboard.

"The dirty bastard," I commented, and Miss Stock looked at me.

"Oh?"

"A friend gone," I said irritably, reaching for the black Daniel's bottle. "Not an old friend. I don't have any old friends . . ." I poured a shot, took it neat, refilled the jigger, and shoved it toward the blond skipper. She took it almost perfunctorily, and set the small glass down.

"Stress, obviously. Can I help?" she asked.

I considered her across the polished bar. For all her brusque mannerisms and habit of command, she was still a womanly woman. Honed fine, tanned and head-strong, but at that age when, if she wanted something, she'd take it with both hands. The hazel eyes met mine with faint derision.

Romany was bending southeastward under full sail. I am not a sailor, but have been, in my travels, close enough to the mystique of it to sense the enormous satisfaction of a well-found ship making its own wind passage. And the people who drive them to it may be the last free tribe in the world . . .

The black-hulled racing yacht was St. Sauteurs-bound. The spice island of the Caribbean, with all the problems it posed for me, was at the end of that wind.

"Your course is set," I told the tall girl. "Your boys can hold a straight helm, so you're out of a job for a few hours. Where are the captain's quarters?"

"Across the companionway from your stateroom," she said quietly.

I nodded. "Could I come to you there?"

"No. They are not really my quarters. Carl is the captain. But I will come to you."

I had another drink, and threw my head to one side like a gaffed fish. I was unused to ladies of this quality, with such original honesty. "Not in the charter, as you said, but it would be a kindness . . ."

She laughed, not very mirthfully. "To solace me, *montressor,* or to forget the *cafè au lait* girl who got pushed over the side?"

"I'm not sure," I said. She shoved the bottle across the rosewood surface and I had another shot from it.

"Why do you keep doing it," she asked, "if it depresses you so much?"

"Doesn't, very often. I'm a retired warrior, and there's not much market for them. Beats selling insurance, smiling for a living. Why do you keep hauling up anchor and clawing off the sight of shore?"

Her answer was quick and decisive. "Because the people on shore are dishonest and tricky. You can breathe at sea, when you don't have to deal with them . . ." She came around the bar and stood next to me, sitting on the high stool.

I hauled up the singlet and kissed the firm, blue-veined breasts, and their aureoled nipples stiffened.

They were salt-flavored. She broke away and left the salon, saying that she had to tell the crew where she could be found. I reached for the bottle of sour mash whiskey and took it back to my stateroom.

In twenty minutes she came to join me, smelling fresh after her shower. Lay for a long time naked, with her head in my right elbow, before we made love. Or rather, demonstrated the dexterity we had learned in handling other questing animals. And that brought several climaxes, the products of kinetic skills rather than emotions, but it was a sudden summer storm just the same. *Nothing barred, in a complete release . . .*

Afterward, as *Romany* went down the long beat to St. Sauteurs, she cried quietly in my arms. For an undone dream or two, and the fact that we were so wise and proficient in fornication, and so lacking in love . . .

While she wept, I was thinking how I must prevent the banker-type from being harmed in St. Sauteurs.

We put into St.George's

harbor at St. Sauteurs, about three the next afternoon. This famous harbor was created long ago when one volcanic wall collapsed. It is completely protected, can accommodate large-draft vessels at its principal pier, and has the largest and busiest yacht marina in the Caribbean. Its picturesque villas, public buildings, and stores rise in handsome tiers around the waterfront, and are an astonishing sight when approached from the sea. St. George's is the loveliest small harbor in the world.

After *Romany* was berthed in the marina, I was passed routinely through customs and immigration since I was listed on her crew. I borrowed $200 Biwee from Martha Stock, as a charge against the charter, and caught a cab to the golf club. This was a nine-hole layout high above Grand Anse Beach, and in it the agency kept a "safe" apartment on an annual basis.

It was no pitch-and-put course. The fairways were

curved, divided by graceful rows of casuarina trees, which have no leaves but needled foilage like mimosa. When a gentle wind blows through them it sings, and a strong wind makes them whistle. Across the high bowl the course was in, the trade winds usually had them whistling. With thirteen tees, you could play eighteen holes, and if your ball found the rough, you needed a cutlass to locate it.

The secretary and principal owner of the course was Lt. Col. F. T. J. Browning, retired. He was a slender man, nearly white, with whipcorded muscles, who spoke Cantabrigian and showed me the small, hidden flat on a blind lower terrace of the club. It came out, in our casual talk, that he had been selected for the West Indies cricket team as a lad of sixteen, and was the only scratch golfer on the island.

The entrance to the flat was entirely separate from the front entrance to the golf club, down a side stairway that dead-ended before its entrance. As I walked into it, I realized with astonishment that the place was a self-sufficient, small fortress. It had all the amenities, a well-appointed kitchen with refrigerator and stove bought in England, and a front side with all bullet-proof, adjustable glass louvres.

The door, or rather the whole wall opening onto the terraced entrance, was also glass-louvred doors of the same quality, with heavy steel frames and grilles. Colonel Browning went around slamming the glass louvres closed, and switched on the air conditioning system, which blasted cold air through the three small rooms.

"Lovely," I said, "but it can also be lethal, if someone drops a cyanide egg into it from outside. Then it becomes a cage."

"Observe, please!" Colonel Browning flipped another switch, and blower fans cleared the apartment in a few seconds. He explained that "my chaps" had brought

their own blueprints down five years ago and supervised construction, and that he was free to rent the flat
on a short-term basis, providing it could be available
immediately, when the agency needed it.

I said that sounded fair, and he went bounding back
up the dead-end stairway. After showering, I checked
the refrigerator and found it well stocked, including a
plate of recently made club sandwiches. I wolfed down
two of them, with two glasses of chilled milk from
paper cartons, and went back up the side stairs after
locking the vaultlike doors.

The car that Colonel Browning had promised me was
waiting, a trim Vauxall sedan with a driver. We drove
back down the steep hill at the western edge of the
golf course to the road that ran behind Grand Anse
Beach, a long curve of white sand fringed by tall palms,
their tops clotted with coconuts. The sea off the white
beaches was only slightly ruffled with waves, held green
and blue shallows, and small Sunfish sailboats were
bounding across its inshore waters.

Fred Sisco, the imminent manager of First National
City's emergence in St. Sauteurs, was in his cottage at
the Spice Island Inn. He was a hearty, heavy-shouldered
Yank with a nice blond wife who was being driven
nuts by three rampaging kids under ten. When his wife
had hazed them out to the beach, I discussed the position with Mr. Sisco. He said that he would do whatever
I thought was wise, since he had very little experience
in being kidnapped in foreign countries.

That attitude helped, because he was a fairly rough-
looking character himself, with a nose broken while
playing guard for Cornell. We talked for an hour, and
I said that I would be back at noon the next day to accompany him to Government House in the car the
Prime Minister was sending. He agreed to accept no

other arrangement; we had another rum punch and parted.

I rode back up to my fortress in the golf club in late afternoon. When the car had driven away, I was alone there, because the club did not seem much of a social center after dark. In the fading light, yellow radiance fell across the course below my terrace. To the southeast, I could see a protected bay on the Atlantic side; beyond it, highballing freight train waves were smashing. To the southwest, a view across the south part of Grand Anse Beach and Point Saline, tranquil and curving.

It was to the northwest of my lonely terrace that the view was spectacular. Lights were coming on in St. George's harbor. Row on row, the steep streets bloomed with illuminated terraces, ringing the dark water of the carenage. Forests of masts in the marina pitched gently over lighted portholes. The neon symbols around the harbor were like an incredible strewing of nighttime jewelry . . .

There was a suitcase of

clothes in the fortress apartment, placed there since I had left it. They were all my size, not new, and laundered to show use. I showered again, and discarded the salt-impregnated clothes Ian Mackenzie had given me in Dominica. There was a bottle of Old Oak rum in the fridge, so I had a touch of it. Got out the depleted remains of the sandwich plate and was picking at it, staring out over the moon-washed contours of the golf course, when a queer howling started.

I switched off the single light and listened. The keening lament came from just below the terrace, a drop of thirty feet.

"Good night, darlin'," quavered the voice. "Have a good night, darlin' . . ."

I sat still in the darkened apartment. The wind rustled through it; the eerie cry kept coming.

"Have a good night, darlin' . . ."

Everytime I had thought it ended with the wind whistling through the casuarina trees, the plaintive voice came again. "Night, darlin' . . . "

I stepped out onto the darkness of the terrace. An old Negro crone was standing below, baskets and reed-woven hats balanced on her head, sad Gullah lips sagged to madness. She had been out all day, walking the beaches without success, and had stopped by to serenade the light in the clubhouse. She could not see me and finally went trudging off toward the hills, still shouting . . .

An hour later, I was reading the *Newsweek* I had picked up in the club's card room upstairs, when I heard a car come up the hill to the west and start around the edge of the deserted course. I switched off my lights and went out on the terrace. The car stopped up above me in front of the clubhouse, cut its lights, and an elderly black man came down the side steps toward my apartment. He was carrying a long box.

He put the box down and peered into the dark apartment. When I said "yes?" from the shadows, he was startled and jerked toward me.

"Who are you?" I asked.

"Robin, sir. The tailor from Parish Street in St. George's."

I stepped past him and flipped the lights on inside the apartment. "What have you got in the box, Robin?"

He grunted, lugging the box inside. "Enough to get me ten long years in that prison on the hill, was I caught with it . . ." Kneeling, still agitated, the old Negro with the fringe of gray hair took the top off the box and handed the weapons up to me for inspection. Two carbines, a light machine gun, two machine pistols. Plenty of ammo. When I had checked the actions on all of them, I nodded acceptance and the agitated tailor asked if he could go.

When I nodded, he hurried back up the stairs and I stood listening to his car hum around the course again. He was driving too fast for a man who did not want attention, but he felt impelled to put distance between himself and the contraband weapons.

I checked them over again, loaded them, and put the box in the bathroom. It took me another half hour to finish the news magazine; then I brushed my teeth and locked the vaultlike steel door to the terrace, but kept the glass louvres open. The trade winds from the northeast blew constantly through the apartment, sometimes gusting, and harped a whistling sibilance through the casuarinas.

As I settled down to sleep, several mosquitoes began droning around my ears and I slapped at them ineffectively. Getting up, I searched the kitchen closet for an aerosol insecticide. There was none, but from the closet shelf I picked a six-inch square box that brought back old memories of India and Burma. The gaudy red box showed a green coil, some defunct mosquitoes with their legs in the air, and was labeled *"GLOBE MOSQUITO DESTROYER."* Manufactured by the Earth Chemical Co., Ltd., Japan.

The damned things worked, too. There was a cheap tin stand inside and, after you had impaled one of the serpentine green rings on its prong and lighted the tip, it smoked like a punk, slowly, for five or six hours. They worked because the principal ingredient was pyrethrin, which was also used in the modern aerosol insecticides. I found other smudged tin stands on a shelf in the bathroom, and lighted up three of the little green snakes. The mosquitoes went away, and I went to sleep.

But not for long. Because I am an incontinent man and drink far too much, my bladder forces me awake every two or three hours. It was well after midnight when I swung my legs off the bed, glanced at the moon-lit terrace, and froze.

Someone was sitting there, motionless, on the loung-ing chair. Not ten feet away from me, just beyond the massive door and the opened glass louvres. *Not John Ratoon; that was the first check I made.* A thick-bodied man, a big man. His bare feet at the end of the lounge chair held thonged sandals, and his muscular legs were tanned. Above the knees, he was in shadow and seemed to be watching not the apartment, but the moon-lit golf course. *A white man . . .*

I stepped barefooted into the bathroom and as noise-lessly as possible took one of the loaded machine pis-tols from the case. My swollen bladder was forgotten in professional indignation. *This indolent bastard had moved in on me with ease, while I slept, and could have blown my head off.* That fact would have been fairly newsworthy, too; a dead Yank with an apartment full of illegal weapons.

When I took the machine pistol off safety, there was a slight click and I waited. When nothing happened, I stepped back out and put the muzzle of it through the waist-high, open space of the glass louvres.

"Get up slowly," I instructed the intruder, "keeping your hands well above your head. If you do anything else I'll saw you right in two."

The thick-bodied figure moved, but did not get up. "My dear chap," it said jovially. "If I do that, might spill my drink, y'know."

I squeezed the trigger. The big pistol jumped, a slug scorched off the tile under his lounge chair and went into a screaming ricochet off the terrace ledge.

"Now do it," I said.

The thick-bodied figure sighed, got off the lounge chair, and put a tall glass down on the terrace edge. tinkled in the glass. Then, leisurely, the figure raised both arms, and I recognized both the flaring skirts of the bush jacket and the indolent voice.

Unlocking the ponderous door, I stepped outside, patted him down, and ordered him inside. My guest was Colonel Peter Frampton, my old friend and fellow passenger on the *Federal Palm.* When I flipped on the lights, he sank into one of the big chairs and beamed at me.

"Really, old chap," he admonished. "You have a vile temper. I was only admiring the view."

"Colonel," I said wearily, "what the hell do you want?"

"Best explained over a drink, y'know," he beamed. "Just step outside, and get mine . . . "

"You'll just sit there on your Perfidious Albion ass until I know why you copped a sneak on me." Carrying the pistol, I moved past him into the kitchen and opened the refrigerator. "Still Cockade rum, I suppose?"

"Ah, good show, old man!" chortled the colonel. I broke out an ice tray, opened a bottle of soda, and took two glasses and a chilled bottle of the Barbados rum to the table beside him. My drink was moderate; his herculean and untainted by soda. "Cheers," he said, and slugged at it.

"So?"

He looked at his wristwatch, on a thick wrist that was more rusted than tanned. "There'll be a floor show in St. George's in about twenty minutes," he announced. "Thought you ought to see it. That's why I didn't waken you. No need, really, 'til the show starts."

"What kind of show?"

"Some bad hats are going to burn down an appreciable section of the mercantile establishment in St. George's," he said, sounding not at all drunk. "Call them, if you will, malcontents, scofflaws, members of the Mongoose Gang."

"That's the P.M.'s security outfit, isn't it?"

"Right. Five of the leading stores will be burnt down. They are all owned by Syrians."

"But . . . " I was trying to digest it. "But there's still time . . . "

Colonel Frampton laughed. "Oh, no. Not my bloody island, y'know. And I'm pressed for time. Staying with some yachting types at L'ance aux Epines, and we push off before dawn. Barbados way. But I thought you ought to see the fires."

I strengthened my drink and stared at "Petah" Frampton closely. He had shed all the ramping mannerisms that had made me sure he was a public-school-type queer. And he seemed to know more about my business than I did, which vexed me. Still, he could have killed me while I slept.

I dressed, if putting on a short-sleeved sport shirt, shorts, and sandals can be called dressing. After I had locked the heavy door behind us and we were going up the stairs, I saw that he had cadged the almost-full bottle of Cockade rum and remarked on it. He replied simply that rum was the wine of warriors, and that he was an old one. I would surely forgive him.

I replied that since I hadn't paid for it, I would. At the top of the stairs, parked before the entrance to the clubhouse, was a white Sprite with no top. Both of us stepped into it without opening the doors, and the colonel took off like a bomb. The noise of our passage whined across the moonlit valley and the empty fairways.

We went racketing toward St. George's along the sweeping curves of the highway above Grand Anse Beach. It was perceptibly hotter, even at that hour, than it had been up in the high valley where the golf course was located. We made no attempt to talk because that was impossible in the wind-rush, but every few miles Frampton had a belt out of the bottle.

At the outskirts of St. George's, he turned into an upward road, and we went humming between dark rows of houses. Only a few lights glinted on the dark harbor water down below, and at the marina all the masted vessels were battened down. When we were high above the harbor, Colonel Frampton braked the little sports car into an overlook and cut the motor.

We waited for an hour with an unobstructed view of the tiered harbor city, but nothing happened. Then, beyond the tunnel that separated the carenage side from the market side, a glow mounted, and smoke started pouring from a building we could not see.

"De Freitas and Sons," said Frampton, stabbing with a finger. "Import-export, groceries, liquor store, and apartments."

The fiery stain grew larger; smoke plumed from it. On the carenage side, two other fires started. Then a fourth. Sirens sounded, and from the fire station near the wharf, the engines rolled out with flashing red lights.

"They'll do fuck-all," announced Colonel Frampton moodily. "The poor sods would be better to piss on the flames. They don't have enough pressure to begin putting them out."

I took the bottle away from him, and had a short belt myself. He seemed well-versed on all aspects of St. Sauteurs' life and institutions.

The fires mounted. Sirens screamed, lights went flashing on around the harbor, and people began to enter the deserted streets below. But there were still only four fires. Frampton said that one attempt must have fizzled; he started the car, and we went humming back the way we had come.

When we were almost back to the golf club, with

the little white car racketing its passage off mango groves and stilt-supported huts, Frampton shouted to me that the "sods" were going to make a snatch attempt on our banker chap tomorrow. On his way to Government House.

"Wouldn't try the Grand Anse road with him," he advised in a modulated roar. "But there's only the other way, through the plantations. Fearful road, that. They'll probably have ambushes on both routes. You must blast the bastards, you know. Because if they get him and demand a ransom, this bloody government will stall and he'll get murdered."

We swept around the western perimeter of the golf course, silvered with moonlight, and the colonel had the tires wailing. He was the noisiest agent I had ever encountered. Tearing off more rubber as he whipped the small car to a sliding halt before the darkened clubhouse, he had another belt out of the Cockade rum bottle.

"Why will they kill him?" I asked.

"Because," he said impatiently, "these blokes can't pay for last week's wash. And it's a small island; they can't hide him. Before you could get the money from the States, he'd be dead."

"Do you know John Ratoon?"

"Much better than I know you. He's the man behind it all. The revolt, the fires tonight, the snatch that will be attempted tomorrow."

I stepped out of the white sports car without opening the door. "Colonel," I said, "I'm indebted to you. My thanks."

"Nothing," he answered. Had another slug out of the bottle of Cockade rum, and settled it on the leather upholstery beside him.

"Besides which," I said politely, "you are one of the

best actors in the world, bar not Olivier. That act on the *Federal Palm,* as a ramping queer, was flawless."

"Is it so?" he asked, beaming. "But then, none of us are what we seem, are we?" He started the waspish motor of the sports car. Over its uproar he shouted, "Please tell your Pearsall hello for me. I knew him long ago in the Greek Isles, where burning Sappho loved and sung . . . "

I nodded; he raised a hand in parting salute and tried to tear the tires off the sports car as he scorched it around and went humming back toward the beach road. I walked down the stairs, unlocked the heavy door, and locked myself in again.

I had a late breakfast

the next morning, sitting on the shaded terrace. Sipping my coffee, grown on the island, I watched large white sea birds stalking jerkily through the high grass rough of the golf course, and thought about the antic Englishman. The prancing colonel who had foreknowledge of arson in St. Sauteurs.

He had not been mentioned in my instructions, and his only connection with the agency was his mention of Pearsall's name. Down below the terrace, a black boy on a motorcycle was herding goats off the course; he had his machine wheeling and swerving like a cutting horse . . . I decided I wouldn't worry about the flamboyant Englishman because I didn't have time to reach the yacht and check him out by radio-telephone.

Just after twelve o'clock, I carried the long box with the loaded weapons in it up the side stairs and put it in the back of Browning's black sedan. After I explained to the driver that I wanted to go to the Spice Island Inn, but not along the beach highway, he nodded and said we could take a circular route to the south, by the sugar mill, and approach the hotel from the other side.

The narrow roadway led through St. David's Parish, and was fringed by low red and yellow croton bushes and towering ceiba and saman trees. The voluble driver kept running on about how someone had tried to burn St. George's down last night, five fires in the heart of town. I kept murmuring "oh?" and "that a fact?" and when my rectal sphincter twitched again, I cursed and told him to stop. Then I fought my way through the underbrush to a slight clearing, hunkered down, and relieved myself with a rush. Thinking it was a fine goddamned time to have dysentery hit.

A few miles farther down the road, we passed several poor shacks made of tin and thatch and I ordered the driver to stop again. Sitting on the sagging step of the nearest hut was something out of a nightmare or a Grimm fairy tale. And two small children just like her came running around the dilapidated hut. Albino Negroes. Queer creatures with parchment-white skin, pink eyes, and snowy, kinky polls absolutely devoid of pigment. Even their eyelashes were white.

When I waved, the driver drove slowly on, laughing. He said that there were quite a few of "those fellows" on the island, and that they grew angry when you said they were white. Howled that they were black people, like everybody else.

"Are they retarded?" I asked. "I mean, simpleminded?"

"No sah. Have one in secondary school, quite bright. He argue with you, fight with you. But they have a complex about it, I think."

Remembering the thick, pale lips and snowy top-knots, I could understand why. We passed the sugar mill, which was thundering away, and drove along the stream where its liquid residues emitted an incredible stench. A ramshackle, gaudily painted bus with the brave name, *"Study Your Head!"* crowded us off the road as it roared by, and then we passed Westerhall Point, L'ance aux Epines, and approached the Spice Island Inn from the south side.

It was still an hour before we were to leave for Government House, but Prime Minister Ferrê's dark green Chevrolet was already there. The driver wore a dark suit, a black chauffeur's cap, and looked a little muscle-bound. When I had transferred the box of weapons to the back seat of his official car, I tipped Browning's driver and told him I would get a taxi back to the clubhouse.

There were three taxis parked nearby with drivers lounging in them, so I walked the P.M.'s man away, over to the shade under the horizontal branches of the almond trees. His name was Octave Leo, and when I explained the position, his heavy black face was first puzzled, and then dubious. I kept on talking, assuring him that if I had alerted the government, they would have had the hotel and the whole highway to St. George's bristling with troops, firing wildly at each other. And probably, us.

That I wanted him to sit in the back seat with the American banker, Mr. Sisco, and be prepared to use a carbine on anybody who attempted to block our passage, or remove Mr. Sisco from the car. Did he know how to use a carbine? He nodded, and said he always kept one in the car. At all times. I said fine, that gave us an extra one.

He was still dubious, thumbing his flattened nose, and said he could get fired if anything went wrong. I asked what would happen to him if a distinguished guest of the government of St. Sauteurs, in his charge, was kidnapped and possibly killed? That such things had happened recently, in several Caribbean and Central American countries, notably the murder of the German ambassador to Guatemala, Count von Spreti.

Yes, he had read about that. *But he was supposed to drive the government car, mon! It was what they paid him for.* I replied that I had a great advantage over him; that I knew where the ambushers would hit us, and that I was a professional racing car driver, or had been, in the United States. This was a lie of purest ray serene, but the bulky black man considered it gravely. After I had peeled off a number of bank notes with impressive numbers on them, he decided my plan would work. He would sit in the back with Mr. Sisco while I drove.

As the lounging taxi drivers stared, I got behind the wheel of the dark green government car, and Octave Leo went into the hotel to get the American banker. While I was waiting, I tested the clutch, brake pressure, and the spring tension on the accelerator, hoping I could remember to stay on the wrong side of the road.

Fred Sisco came striding out of the hotel lobby in a dark tropical suit and tie, nodded to me, and ducked into the back seat. Octave got in beside him, and we swung around and back down the road toward St. George's. We went humming by the open, treeless acres dotted with modern cottages, put up two years ago for St. Sauteur's Caribbean Exposition, and stopped just short of the main road. We were still in sight of some of the cottages, but that couldn't be helped.

Leaning back, I flipped the top of the box, handed Fred Sisco a machine pistol, and showed him the safety. Since he had been in the Marine Corps for two years, a lieutenant in Vietnam, I knew he would have no trouble with it. Octave wanted his own carbine from the floor of the front seat, and got it; I plucked a carbine from the case and put it on the front seat beside me.

Then, looking straight ahead and gesturing, I laid down the fields of fire. Emphasizing that if anybody got rattled, and started swing-shooting, we could easily annihilate each other. Thus, Sisco had the right rear 90-degree arc, Octave the left one, and I had the frontal 180-degree fire-field.

They both nodded, and instead of going north along the beach road I swung south toward Point Saline. Leo leaned forward, questioning, and I explained that the ambushers would almost certainly be waiting on the main approach to St. George's. That we were going to double back past the sugar factory and go through St. David's Parish on the plantation road. The black muscleman nodded and leaned back, satisfied with the explanation.

The road was pot-holed and spine-jarring, but the well-tuned car kept accelerating even while its suspension was taking a beating.

We roared past the sugar factory, by its stinking downstream waters, and were smashing through verdure, which kept slapping at the opened, front window vents, when I turned up the narrow mountain road which would bring us into St. George's from the other side.

Both the steering wheel and column were vibrating under my hands when we swept by the parish police station and its cluster of rum shops. As I angled into the next turn, I saw two cars rolling silently down out of the green banana-tree gloom to box us off. As we approached them, I jammed down the accelerator.

"All right, gentlemen," I announced. "This is it. Remember that I can't fire backward, and you can't fire forward."

For a couple of seconds, left hand steadying the wheel and right hand curled around the stock of the carbine, I thought we might get by. Then the car from the left struck our rear fender, and the one coming from above struck us at the right front door.

Black men started spilling out of both cars as the Chevrolet was knocked sideways and into a low retaining wall. They all held weapons, but had to stop their forward motion after tumbling out of moving vehicles. By that time, we three were firing. I got two point-blank and shot one in the face from a distance of two feet. He turned into an astonished flood of blood and sagged out of sight. Behind me, Octave and Banker Sisco were also firing point-blank, and several of the would-be kidnappers broke and ran back toward the protection of the banana-plants across the road.

I put the Impala in the grandma hole, poured the power to it, and shunted the kidnap cars aside. One assassin had not quit. He was sprawled on the hood of the car, clinging to it perilously and aiming a .45-caliber pistol straight at my head. I wrenched the steering wheel hard, one side and the other, while his shots starred the windshield. The car was gathering speed, I was savaging the wheel, and he was sliding off.

When another jerk sent him over the left fender, I shifted the carbine and emptied it into him as he fell. Tufts of his shirt and flesh jumped as the slugs plowed into him, and he screamed with agony as his body catapulted against refuse barrels, bounced, and lay quivering in death.

Sisco and Octave were still firing behind me, but there must have been at least one patriot left. With a rifle. I heard three sharp cracks, lighter than the other firing, and somebody said "anngh!" and moaned. I kept the accelerator down, to get out of range of the rifle.

"Who got hit?" I asked sharply, sweeping the curve ahead.

"Mr. Sisco, sir."

I flashed a backward glance. Sisco was bent forward; I could not see any wound. Kept ramming the car toward St. George's. Two turns later, after he had groaned again, I had another quick look. His white shirt was stained with blood. I braked the car and pulled off into the first place where the road was wide enough. Jumped out and told Octave to get behind the wheel, and to take us to the emergency ward of Colony Hospital. Then I got in the back seat.

Sisco was curled almost into the fetal position, and said in a clear voice that he thought the shot might have gone through his lung. If so, he was in bad shape. I removed his blood-soaked coat, and started tearing the white shirt off. There was a small, bluish hole high in the back where the slug had entered, but I could not find any place where it had left.

That bothered me because it did not explain where the blood was coming from, and there was a lot of it. He had not bled from the mouth. Yet he was hemorrhaging somewhere. In the speeding car, I could not find out where. My rectal sphincter throbbed again, all I needed, and I said "nuts to you" and locked my bowels.

After I had helped Octave carry him into the emergency room, we had a bad time while the duty nurse stripped him and fiddled around. I finally raised enough hell, and we got a mulatto doctor who took over with cool competence. Then I sat on a hard bench outside for half an hour, until the doctor came out and said that Sisco's wound was through muscular tissue. That he would be quite all right after transfusions to replace the blood loss and several days of rest.

After assuring him that any expenses incurred, of private room or medication, would be met by the United States government, the *café au lait* doctor said that nothing drastic was involved. Mr. Sisco had a superficial wound, and would soon be up and around again. I thanked him, and arranged for guards around the clock at the banker's door.

Octave drove me to Government House. After we had gone through the imposing gates and stopped before the large building, I got out and went inside. Asked for the Prime Minister, and got his secretary. It was, perhaps, a matter he could handle, suggested the handsome young mulatto.

I explained about the unfortunate incident, saying that several of the ambushers were dead, others wounded, and that Mr. Sisco, the American banker, had received a superficial wound. He was presently in Colony Hospital, and hence would not be able to keep the appointment with His Excellency. But would, of course, seek another one when he recovered.

The dapper secretary registered shock. "I'm sure the P.M. will be most distressed, an assault on a distinguished visitor. We will see that he gets the best of care . . . " He hesitated. "And your name, sir?"

"Joseph Miles, an associate of Mr. Sisco's. I have already arranged a guard for his room at the hospital, and I wonder if the government could provide one for his wife and children? They're staying at the Spice Island Inn."

"Immediately," he said. "Please convey our deepest regrets to Mrs. Sisco, and tell her to ring the P.M. direct if she needs anything."

"Thank you," I said. We shook hands formally, and he turned and walked briskly back down the long hallway.

I walked back out across

the columned portico, but Octave and the government
car were gone, and I suspected he had taken it around
to the garage. To count the bullet holes. Quite a few
had chinked into it. I was walking down the curved
gravel drive toward the gates, sweating in the midafter-
noon glare, when two large buses entered the grounds
and forced me onto the grass.

They stopped in a shower of gravel before Government House, and began to discharge black U.S. paratroopers in full battle dress. They wore jump boots
which were so highly polished that the sun struck sparks
from them, and combat decorations, and had sidearms
and submachine guns. Ammo bandoliers were strung
across their shoulders. Their dark officers sported
canted berets and formed them up with incisive orders.
Spit-and-polish, and esprit de corps as ever was . . .

While I watched standing beside the St. Sauteurs sentry at the entrance gates, the mulatto secretary I had spoken to, Prime Minister Eric Ferré, and several other high government officials came out and stood on the steps. Standing stiffly, they received the salute from the two black paratroop platoons, by hand from the officers and by pieces rattled to the order from the troops.

Beside me, the sentry murmured with awe, "Mon, ain't them boys do it *fine!*" and I could not repress a nod of pride. As an old military lag, I knew they were doing it as smartly as any West Pointers could. And the best was yet to come.

Wheeling rearward to the order, the two black platoons went off the gravel drive onto the tended sward and began an accelerated close-order drill. Both the ranks and the officers were chanting in syncopated unison as they doubled back flawlessly, bounced their weapons off the grass, and strutted in balletic precision.

"Had a good home, but I *LEFT!*" And they wheeled left and flourished their arms in a graceful cartwheel from their elbows. Took another step and wheeled back the other way, with an agility seldom seen in St. Sauteurs. And I knew how tough it was to make the maneuvers on grass. First, because they were usually done on asphalt or concrete parade grounds, where you could get more contact with the grounded weapons; and secondly because the short automatic pieces they were carrying were harder to balance than their usual rifles.

For twenty minutes they went through this precise, swinging exercise, while shouts and applause came from the crowd which had gathered in front of Government House. The Prime Minister, Ferré, a stocky, frog-faced black man, was smiling with delight, and so were his ministers and aides. Finally, the two platoons wheeled back on the gravel before the portico and stamped their boots to a halt.

Standing at ramrod attention, eyes fixed forward, they listened to their black major read the inscription on a mahogany plaque bearing an inscribed gold plate, conveying the greetings of the United States of America to the government of St. Sauteurs, West Indies, and assuring that government of the best wishes . . .

Prime Minister Ferré stepped forward, accepted the plaque, and made several remarks to the braced U.S. Major of Paratroops. I could not hear what he said, and when he began to pass down the line, shaking hands with the individual paratroopers, I walked out of the grounds and down toward the center of St. George's. I had to go several blocks before I found a cab, and on my way down the cobbled road I reflected. *No half-assed revolutionary party was going to take over this government while those combat-trained platoons with the perfect cadence and grenades hanging off them like steel mangos were in town* . . .

I went back by the hospital and found Sisco with his forearm taped to a board, getting a transfusion. He was pale, but managed to joke, and said that the frigging slug had glanced off his rib cage. Made its exit in his left armpit, and that was why I hadn't been able to locate the source of the bleeding. His principal concern, of course, was for his family, so I told him about the guard on his room and the government's promise of a guard for them.

When he said he was grateful to me, and what could he do in repayment, without any expression I said what could any banker do? Lower his goddamned interest rates . . . When I walked out, he was laughing, and I suppose it was a joke of sorts.

After the cab let me out at the golf club, I went down to the fortress apartment and had another session on the thunder throne because the dysentery was still bothering me. After another shot of bismuth and paregoric,

I went back up the side stairway and asked Colonel Browning for the use of his car. He granted it, and we went back toward the Spice Island Inn the long way, through St. David's Parish.

It was late afternoon as we lurched along the narrow road, past nutmeg groves and purple cocoa pods growing directly out of the trunks. Towering groves of bamboo arched above us, like green frond-fountains frozen in place, and hibiscus, frangipani, and anthurium lilies bloomed in riotous profusion. No one was in sight when we passed the huts of the albino Negroes, but the stench downstream from the sugar mill was as bad as before.

At the Spice Island Inn I went to Mrs. Sisco's bungalow and comforted her as much as I could. She was composed, and while we talked the children rampaged around us. I told her about the guards, and she said yes, one had already arrived. She pointed him out through the glass louvres in the front of the cottage. He was leaning on the beach bar, chatting up a black bird in a bikini, and would obviously be of as much value as tits on a boar hog.

Mrs. Sisco was an attractive and cared-for woman, a brisk blond type, and I wondered what several years of residence on a hot island like St. Sauteurs would do to her Junior League background, which seems to involve a certain sterility. After I had left her, I braced the guard at the beach bar, and said that if he could keep no closer watch than he was doing at present, he might as well leave. And that I had just left Prime Minister Ferré, and would report his dereliction.

He was a big, gap-toothed black man, and heard me out with astonishment. Put down his glass of rum punch, and said, "Mon, you upsettin' youself to no purpose. I watch the foreign lady like a hawk. No possible harm come to she!"

"Good," I answered, and went walking north along the beach under the arching palms. It was heavy going, so I took off my shoes and socks, and dropped down to the border of wet sand. As I passed the Riviera Hotel, I noticed two small black boys piling sand on another one. The buried boy was walling his eyes, and only his head was uncovered. I got several paces past this horse-play before I realized that the buried boy had an enormous head.

Pausing at the beach road between the Riviera and the Silver Beach Hotels, I glanced back. The two small black boys were piling sand on the stomach of the one with the abnormally large head. They made a huge mound of it. I retreated to stand beside them.

"See!" shouted one of the frolicking boys, "he's pregnant."

"A shame," I commented. "Who is responsible for this outrage?"

The two black boys capered with glee at this imputation of parentage, and the grinning black head broke its bondage of sand. Got up shaking like a dog, and became Timothy George, the black dwarf.

"Give us a quarter, boss," he demanded, and I pieced the three of them off, quarter, quarter, quarter. With no thanks given, the trio ran laughing up the road between the two luxury hotels, the bandy-legged dwarf lurching from side to side. On the way they stopped to hurl juice nuts, fallen coconuts in their green pods, at each other.

I walked on to the thatched hut beyond the Silver Beach, where speedboat rides, water-skiing trips, and glass-bottomed excursions were for sale. There I paid a Nordic type with long, flaxen, sunbleached hair for three hour's use of his cruiser. It took me around Point Saline, southernmost point on St. Sauteurs, to *Romany Two*.

Martha Stock gave me a kiss on boarding, and I returned it with considerable emphasis. We went below, and I had her place a call to Neal Pearsall in Washington, but we were informed by the big agency station that he was out of the office. There would be an hour's delay. We spent that hour in pleasant dalliance at the bar, drinking sour mash whiskey. I trying to remove her brassiere while we conversed, and she slapping me off half-heartedly.

When all this nonsense was about to become bedborne, Neal checked in. Booming through the receiver like a ton of bricks. He was in Barbados, in the Hilton Hotel, having come down to supervise the visit of the black U.S. paratroopers to the Caribbean Islands. As before, after the initial contact Martha put me on an earphone contact with a hand mike, and retired to the deck.

I told him about the unsuccessful ambush, and the jaunty drill team of the two platoons at Government House. He said that was good, but not enough. The fellow I had braked off the hood of the Chevrolet and shot to death was Ratoon-Ahmed's brother. By name, Rafer, aged nineteen. He had also been a minor part of the Trembling Earth conspiracy in south Georgia.

As to the take-over, all the smaller Caribbean Islands except St. Vincent had been given a guest guard of armed U.S. paratroopers, all black. One of the Globemasters delivering the troops had developed a malfunction in Barbados, but would land in St. Vincent the next morning, before any commercial flight arrived.

"You've done well, Joseph," summed up Pearsall. "I'm in a suite at the Barbados Hilton. Why not have *Romany* bring you here, and we'll have a few belts and tell each other some gorgeous lies.

"We've checked our permanent contacts on Montserrat, Dominica, St. Vincent, St. Lucia, and St. Sau-

teurs. The arms caches have been located, and most of
the potential saboteurs jailed. You were right about the
black platoons; nothing adverse has appeared about
their visits in any of the local island papers, even those
of the opposition, and so far nothing has been filed by
any news services. We've checked the local stories in
type but not printed, and most of them treat the paratroopers' presence as just another ceremonial visit. So
I guess we're home free."

I listened to the waves wash against *Romany's* sides;
she was pitching gently.

"No, pappy," I said slowly. "I've been this guy's
nemesis twice. Ahmed-Ratoon, I mean. He's a bitter-
ender, this cat, and he'll be after me for the rest of his
life. He's already burned my house half-down and
killed a guest of mine. And now I've killed his brother.
. . . One way or another, he'll keep coming. So I'd
better be where he can find me."

There was a pause on the radio-telephone connection. Finally Pearsall said, "You're going beyond
agency business now."

"That's right. I'll wait for him here in St. Sauteurs."

"Not in the contract," said Pearsall.

"Fuck the contract. It's got to be finished, or he'll
show up again someplace else."

There was another pause on the line; it rashed with
static.

"I'll be here," said Pearsall, "until I hear from you
again. But from now on, it's just vendetta, isn't it?"

"Bet your goddamned life," I said, and jerked the
jack out of the panel.

The dinghy put me

ashore in late afternoon on the far side of the Spice
Island Inn. In front of that elegant hostelry, I got a
taxi and was driven up in the hills to the deserted country club. There was never anyone there after dark, except on Friday nights when a bridge club met. After I
had showered, I sat out on the terrace in jockey shorts
and watched the rows of graceful casuarina trees bending before the breeze.

The sun had plunged below the Caribbean horizon
to the west, and the blue green water had turned slaty.
The smaller bay to the southeast was glinting with
breakers from the Atlantic, and to the north in circular
tiers of lights, was St. George's. A forest of masts and
spars thrust up from the marina. *Romany Two* would
be tying up there soon.

Somewhere across the darkening course an idiot
rooster began crowing, and I concluded that his clock

was off, or he was just practicing. An immense red gold moon broke up over the eastern hills, so huge it looked unreal, and clouds of fireflies sparked the tropic night. Their cold light winked across the course and went with the wind toward Grand Anse Beach.

I was kneeling to unhook the steel door when my right sandal scuffed against something. I cradled a match flame in cupped hands. It was a box about eight inches long and four wide, with a gaudy label. *"GRANT'S SUPERIOR CANDLES,"* made by Trinidad Wax Products, Ltd. There was a string around the box. I took it into the darkened flat, thinking that Colonel Browning had left it for me in case of a power cut-off or failure, which were common in St. Sauteurs.

That possibility didn't concern me at present, however, because I had no intention of turning on any lights. I closed and locked the heavy fortress door, leaving the glass louvres open, and sat down in one of the big chairs. Stripping the carbine in the faintly reflected light of the rising moon, I oiled it, wiped it down, and when it was reassembled, checked the action. When the clip had gone in securely, I canted the light weapon against the side of the chair.

The rising moon was paling to yellow, and it threw moving shadows behind the blowing casuarinas. The demented rooster was still practicing, so urgently I was sure he would give himself a hernia and be useless by dawn. I felt uneasy, couldn't sit still, and seemed to smell something malign in the rustling wind. Most tropic winds are freighted with stenches and jasmine fragrances, but there was something else blowing in this one . . .

Sulfur . . . That was it. I imagined I could smell sulfur. My left ankle, cicatriced with wounds from the forgotten Korean War, began to throb. The right eardrum I had ruptured in a plane crash years ago began to twinge and ache; I pinched my nostrils together and blew into them with my mouth closed. *No relief; the pressure was still there.* Low clouds came scudding over the eastern hills, casting more shadows across the course . . .

Man, you're spooking! I chided myself but lost the argument. I was. *Something baleful was working on me.* Arising, I went into the dark kitchen and got the box of candles that had been on my doorstep.

Knelt, facing away from the front windows, and snapped the string on the box. Lighted one of the flimsy matches made in Czechoslovakia, and the treacherous Communist bastard flared a stinging particle onto my left wrist and went out. Cursing, I struck another and cradled its yellow flame in cupped hands.

The box held the severed head of a huge fer-de-lance. The eyes set in the wedge-shaped head had gone dim, and the elliptical black pupils were sightless. The enormous fangs, still pointed forward, had spewed yellow venom on the sides of the box. The deadly liquid had stained the cardboard.

Two drops, I thought: *death for a man, in a few minutes . . .*

Putting the top back on the box, I dropped the weird gift into the wastebasket. Put on a sport shirt and slung a bandolier of carbine clips over my shoulder. Went back through the dark, quiet apartment for the weapon. Because I knew now for certain what I had thought would be true before.

John Ratoon, late Ahmed 4 of the U.S., was waiting out in the windy moonlit night below me, to avenge his brother.

With some queer sense of tropic punctilio, he had borrowed a custom of the country and warned me, both of his presence and his intention to destroy me. In *obeah,* the African witchcraft practiced in all these hot islands, delivering a fer-de-lance's head in a box placed on the victim's doorstep was part of an old ritual.

Unlocking the heavy door of the terrace apartment, staying in shadow, I gauged the drop-off to the side slope. The terrace there was fringed by high oleander bushes, with clusters of hibiscus just beyond them, on steeply sloping ground. Holding the carbine muzzle up by my right ear, I studied the possible pitfalls of the jump. It was the only way out; going over the front of the terrace meant a drop of thirty feet and would expose me in full moonlight.

The jitters had departed because I was no longer dealing with something unknown. I was still tense, on the high line, but the issue had been joined. *Ratoon was out there, waiting, and had served notice on me.* His bid for a spectacular Caribbean revolt had failed. With the exception of St. Vincent, he had no chance to take over the islands tomorrow morning. And St. Vincent was so poor and out of the way that no one would pay much attention if his people there briefly grabbed the government and the transport moving through on Sunday morning.

His sole concern, now, was to kill me, because I had butchered his younger brother.

Fair enough. I went across the dark living room and snapped on the tall standing lamp.

Outside in the windy darkness something cracked like a breaking tree limb, and a slug smashed through the lampshade, knocking it and the stand over. As it crashed to the floor, the bulb flared and went out.

Jesus, I thought, *this cat pays off like a slot machine!*

From the floor, with the cool stock of the carbine against my cheek, I realized that Ratoon was using a rifle. Probably with a night-scope. His field of fire put him somewhere in an arc about 100 degrees, maximum, to the south of me. He was firing from concealment, in clouded moonlight, at a lighted target. To adjust the odds, I had to go out after him.

This black man had invaded my home in the Ozark Mountains. He and his black troopers had burned that home, wounded me, and killed a visitor of mine. They had been directly responsible for the deaths of my three rare white tigers. So, on this hot island of St. Sauteurs one of us had to die. *We had come to the killing ground* . . .

When I went lunging out of the apartment and over the terrace, he fired at me again. The slug whined off masonry and went ricocheting into space. I landed heavily on the slope, bruising my right elbow but holding the carbine high, and scrambled to the cover of the casuarina trees. Crouched there, listening and raking around for some sign of him.

The ninth green was a high, sloping terrace behind me, barely visible under dark, scudding clouds. Two hundred yards below was another line of casuarinas, screening the deep ravine which divided the fairways. I moved down that way, crouching, safety off the carbine.

The stalk was on. For an hour, seeking shadows, I crouched and moved, listened and waited, moved to another dark covert and waited again. The stock of the carbine was sweaty under my hand. The needled branches of the casuarinas orchestrated the breeze, and bats went wheeling and diving over the fairways.

I grew weary of the game. When a break in the clouds came, plating the course with silvered radiance, I stepped out into the fairway. In full view. The rifle cracked again. Wheeling, I went raking with the carbine.

Ratoon was standing on the high edge of the ninth green. He fired at me again, and missed again, because I was diving. I pressed off another burst just as the ninth green and the hill behind it exploded. Turf, clods, and rock rained down around me, and the hillside began to gout boiling mud with a sulfurous stench. The fairway wrinkled under my feet and began to shudder violently. I was thrown off my feet, and watched in stunned disbelief as the clubhouse went wavering like a picture taken by a palsied man with a hand-held camera.

Scrambling on all fours like an animal, I crossed the quaking ground to where Ratoon had been flung when the green exploded. He was dead enough; my shots had stitched across his face, but only because the quake had flung him into my field of fire. Boiling mud, stinking with scalding sulfur fumes, was gouting out of the hole where the green had been, and I dropped the carbine and went running toward the clubhouse, often falling as the earth billowed under me.

Because the clubhouse was built of stone and cement, it withstood the damage of the earthquake but was still moving. The ditch down in the center of the course had blown open and was spouting fountains of molten mud. I stood braced on the terrace of the apartment and watched a flood of water roar down the slope beside it; the quake had split the big water tower on the hillside above.

The bay on the Atlantic side looked the same. So did the long, palm-fringed white arc of Grand Anse to the west. Then I turned to stare at the harbor in St. George's and was profoundly shocked. At first glance, I thought my eyes had gone wonky on me.

There was no water in the harbor. All the yachts moored in the marina had disappeared!

On the far side of the carenage, I could see the slimy support pilings of the wharves glistening. As I watched in disbelief with the cement floor of the terrace rocking, the water in the harbor came surging back up, boiling and gouting steam. The water churned ten feet above its normal level, engulfing the road, stores, and warehouses. Then dropped as precipitously as it had arisen, sucking down out of sight, freighted with cars, crates, and anything moveable within its terrible suction.

The upward boil of the harbor water had brought the yachts back into view, but only as smashed toys. They were broken and splintered, masts knocked askew, grinding against each other. While I watched, partially in shock, I hoped that Martha Stock was safe. That she had been off the boat, eating at the Nutmeg Bar or out carousing... But it was a slender hope; she loved *Romany* too much, and had probably been polishing the brass.

As I watched, the waters of St. George's harbor dropped out of sight again, and the splintered yachts vanished. I could see only the slimy mud flats. I started running across the golf course, with the ground still trembling under me, and was thrown off my feet twice. When I got down to the beach road, I found it jammed by hordes of dark people moving toward St. George's. Taxis and private cars were trying to honk a way through them with little success.

I knew they were going the wrong way, because I had seen the harbor water boiling up and down, but they didn't know that. St. George's, to them, was the seat of the government, the final hope. They were desperate, a frightened mob, a tidal wave of black people fleeing...

I skirted their frenzy until I found an empty cab, and showed the driver the purity of engraving on a U.S. $100 bank note. He was impressed, and agreed to reverse his direction and drive me through St. David's Parish to Pearls Airport. His name was Cristopher, and fairness impelled him to tell me that there would be no flights from the airport that night.

I assured him that, no matter what the hour was, I would populate the airport. All he had to do was watch for rabid mongooses. He said "sah!" and we went the long way to the airport with the road shaking under us.

When we got to the airport, it took another hour of conversation, two more $100 bills, and some suasion to get the owner of the light-plane charter outfit on deck. I laid a midget ransom on him, he brightened like a morning glory, and we took off for Barbados with the island of St. Sauteurs still shuddering and stinking of hot sulfur.

The arctic blast through

my room in the Barbados Hilton was just like home. So were the prices. I was in the shower when the phone rang, and went dripping to answer it. Neal Pearsall was at the other end.

"You did well, Joseph?" he inquired. He nearly always calls me Joseph, and I always appreciate it. A Biblical streak, I guess. My regard for the man was based on the fact that during all the years I had worked for him, he had been as interested in my personal safety as in the results of my contracts.

"I suppose. He's dead, Neal."

"Splendid! The republic is safe for another half hour.

Will you come have a drink with me? I'm in 2 AA."

"As soon as I dress and complete a call to St. Sauteurs."

"Right." He hung up, and I reflected how unusual it was for him to come down personally to supervise the assignment. In the years I had worked for the agency, he had done that only twice before. It was obvious that Washington had considered this threat of Ratoon's more than ordinarily dangerous. When I was dressed, I had the overseas operator try my call to Colonel Browning again, but she reported that all lines to St. Sauteurs were tied up. I told her I could be reached in 2 AA when the call went through, and walked out to the elevator.

My forty-minute flight to Barbados had been uneventful, but things livened up after I landed at Seawell Airport. Most governments are peckish about the arrival of private planes that land without having filed flight plans, and are especially vexed when the incoming passenger has not cleared customs or immigration at his point of departure. So I was held in a detention room at Seawell for over an hour, vainly protesting that there had been no one at the St. Sauteurs airport to clear with.

When, finally, I had been allowed a phone call to Neal Pearsall, the difficulties vanished with a rush. As I drove to the hotel in a cab, I cherished the solid feel of the roadway, because Barbados has a solid coral foundation, unlike the volcanic substructure of the other Windward Islands.

Pearsall's door opened onto an elaborate foyer, a sitting room, and two bedrooms. As usual, he was flaked out on a double bed, with newspapers strewed all around him and on the floor. Years ago, I had learned a valuable lesson from him; that you could learn more about any given country by reading its want ads and local stories than by visits to its Government House, ministry offices, or embassies. He had instructed me that the price of a used baby carriage was far more important than what officials were saying.

His metal leg was on the other bed, its leather fittings sweat-stained. He had lost the leg from gangrene while lashing troops out of a Korean ambush.

Pearsall was a powerful, overweight man who wore expensive clothes badly; they were always rumpled. He drank nothing but black Jack Daniel's, but since he had Air Force jets at his disposal when traveling, was not troubled by supply. At the side of his bed were two large plastic wastebaskets filled with ice. He routinely carried detergents and scrubbing brushes in his luggage, and when room service sent up their first meager bucket of ice cubes, he scrubbed out the wastebaskets and demanded that they be filled.

I had a belt of the sour mash, and it exploded warmth in my gut. Mostly, I felt relief that I didn't have to watch everything and everybody. Not for a while, at least. Neal said that the Globemaster had landed two black platoons in St. Vincent, so that threat was stopped. I nodded, and told him about the quick-stepping ebony paratroopers I had seen at Government House in St. George's, and a faint smile crossed his heavy bulldog face.

I had another belt, stood up and savaged the tension out of the back of my neck with both hands, and told him they had a bus on the southern run in St. Sauteurs painted like a circus wagon. The name of it was "STUDY YOUR HEAD!" a caution to unwise drivers, of which there were many on that island. But the most interesting feature of this gaudy bus was that its driver had a unique way of deciding which young girls qualified to ride for half-fare.

"Oh?" Pearsall poured out half a glass of black Daniel's and knocked it down straight.

"Yes. He tweaks their tits. Sort of like the weight guesser in a carnival . . ."

Pearsall laughed so hard I thought he would have a heart attack. He choked and whooped, and pounded on the bed with both hands.

"Twelve is the limit for half-fares," I went on, "but girls develop rapidly in this climate, and he claims he can sort them out, within a month or two, by just a nipple-twitch."

He was quaking with glee, beating on the bed. "By God! I love a dedicated man," he roared. "Has a considerable custom, too, I'll bet . . ."

"I'm told his vehicle is packed with nubile, young black girls at all hours," I said, and this sent him off again. "Middle-aged ladies of eighteen or twenty are said to come from the other side of the island. He never misses . . ."

The phone rang, and Pearsall answered it, wiping tears from his eyes. He said, "Yes, just a minute," and held the receiver toward me.

Colonel Browning, the managing director and secretary of the St. Sauteurs Golf Club, was on the line. In clipped tones he said that forty-seven bodies of yachtsmen and crewmen had been recovered from the waters of the carenage in St. George's harbor. But that the total loss was certain to be several times that number. He had not been able to find out anything about Miss Stock, but she was not among the reported dead.

The golf course, he said sadly, was a shocking ruin, but the clubhouse had not been badly damaged, because of its concrete and steel construction. The quakes had subsided, but casualties had overflowed the hospitals, and patients were being placed in schools and churches. I said that if he could find out anything about Martha Stock and help her, dead or alive, I would bear all the expenses. He said he would do it and hung up.

I reported the conversation to Pearsall, and we had another drink, but it tasted flat and unpalatable.

"Peter Frampton, the English bloke, tipped me off about the ambush point," I said finally. "Who the hell is he, and why wasn't I told about him?"

"He's not working for us, although he has. Probably doing a job for Jamaican intelligence. A savvy and courageous man. That blithering-idiot act of his fools people, but he's one of the best. Long ago, when our agency had another name, we worked together in Greece. When George Polk, the CBS newsman, got shot in the head and dumped into Salonika Bay."

"He mentioned that he knew you in Greece."

The air conditioning hummed politely, and Neal poured another half-glass of whiskey. He was in another land, another decade. He slugged it down without changing expression, but seemed to find the drink bitter as aloes.

I told him about finding the severed head of the fer-de-lance in the box on my doorstep. About the moonlit duel on the golf course, where I had been saved by an earthquake. That I had not really caught Ratoon-Ahmed fairly in triggering my carbine, that he had been pitched into the field of fire by the erupting green. The comment brought him back from the past.

"Don't worry about it," he said sharply. "In this business we accept any edge we can get, even an act of God."

Then, because we were both nervous, I told him about the lilac-colored hearse in St. George's, with the louvred windows in the side and the legend, "BON VOY-AGE," painted across the back. Said that I had hoped, if Ratoon chopped me down, to make my last trip in that cheery chariot.

Pearsall relaxed and grinned. "A meat wagon with cross ventilation. Not bad."

We talked on, but I couldn't sustain the light mood. I hadn't eaten, and the bourbon was getting to me.

"One day," I pontificated moodily, "a black Simón Bolívar will arise in these hot islands. These millions of blacks and intermediate shades will become organized. They will look north, toward the United States. Hunger will drive them toward us . . ."

Pearsall sighed, and poured himself another drink. "True, Joseph, but not for another two generations. By then, both of us will be out of action—dead." He belted the drink down and studied the bottom of his empty glass. "Everybody knocks old Ernest Hemingway now, and he did become a caricature of himself there at the last, but he said some important things. He said that the men did not come to die; they came to fight. The dying was accidental . . .

"You and I are old crocks now," he continued quietly, "and most of the 'in' people would not want us as guests for dinner. But we put it on the line when we thought the republic was in danger, in War Two and Korea, and you had the civil revolt in Burma.

"I gave a leg for what I believed in, and you collected a lot of scar tissue in foreign alleys. All we can hope for, if these black islanders do attempt to overrun Nebraska when we are gone, is that there will still be men of our persuasion available, determined to defend that acreage against any invader."

"Look—" I interrupted.

"Don't go on about it!" said Pearsall sharply. "You

did your job; no need to deliver a friggin' editorial."

The big, rumpled man began to strap on his artificial leg. "Let's go downstairs and check on the talent," he said. "I understand it's outstanding, and even dirty old men need affection."

Meet Joe Gall—The Nullifier
in his chilling games
of counterespionage

THE GREEN WOUND CONTRACT R2119 60¢
former title: The Green Wound

THE SILKEN BARONESS CONTRACT R2108 60¢
former title: The Silken Baroness

THE PAPER PISTOL CONTRACT D1975 50¢

THE DEATH BIRD CONTRACT D1886 50¢

THE IRISH BEAUTY CONTRACT D1976 50¢

THE STAR RUBY CONTRACT R2096 60¢

THE ROCKABYE CONTRACT R2228 60¢

THE SKELETON COAST CONTRACT R2322 60¢

THE ILL WIND CONTRACT R2087 60¢

THE TREMBLING EARTH CONTRACT R2181 60¢

by Philip Atlee

"I admire Philip Atlee's writing tremendously, the hard economy of style, the characterizations . . ."—Raymond Chandler

A Fawcett   Gold Medal Book

Wherever Paperbacks Are Sold